ANNE MORICE
KILLING WITH KINDNESS

ANNE Morice, *née* Felicity Shaw, was born in Kent in 1916.

Her mother Muriel Rose was the natural daughter of Rebecca Gould and Charles Morice. Muriel Rose married a Kentish doctor, and they had a daughter, Elizabeth. Muriel Rose's three later daughters—Angela, Felicity and Yvonne—were fathered by playwright Frederick Lonsdale.

Felicity's older sister Angela became an actress, married actor and theatrical agent Robin Fox, and produced England's Fox acting dynasty, including her sons Edward and James and grandchildren Laurence, Jack, Emilia and Freddie.

Felicity went to work in the office of the GPO Film Unit. There Felicity met and married documentarian Alexander Shaw. They had three children and lived in various countries.

Felicity wrote two well-received novels in the 1950's, but did not publish again until successfully launching her Tessa Crichton mystery series in 1970, buying a house in Hambleden, near Henley-on-Thames, on the proceeds. Her last novel was published a year after her death at the age of seventy-three on May 18th, 1989.

BY ANNE MORICE
and available from Dean Street Press

ANNE MORICE

KILLING WITH KINDNESS

With an introduction and afterword by
Curtis Evans

DEAN STREET PRESS

Published by Dean Street Press 2021

Copyright © 1974 Anne Morice

Introduction & Afterword © 2021 Curtis Evans

All Rights Reserved

First published in 1974 by Macmillan

Cover by DSP

ISBN 978 1 914150 03 6

www.deanstreetpress.co.uk

Introduction

By 1970 the Golden Age of detective fiction, which had dawned in splendor a half-century earlier in 1920, seemingly had sunk into shadow like the sun at eventide. There were still a few old bodies from those early, glittering days who practiced the fine art of finely clued murder, to be sure, but in most cases the hands of those murderously talented individuals were growing increasingly infirm. Queen of Crime Agatha Christie, now eighty years old, retained her bestselling status around the world, but surely no one could have deluded herself into thinking that the novel *Passenger to Frankfurt*, the author's 1970 "Christie for Christmas" (which publishers for want of a better word dubbed "an Extravaganza") was prime Christie—or, indeed, anything remotely close to it. Similarly, two other old crime masters, Americans John Dickson Carr and Ellery Queen (comparative striplings in their sixties), both published detective novels that year, but both books were notably weak efforts on their parts. Agatha Christie's American counterpart in terms of work productivity and worldwide sales, Erle Stanley Gardner, creator of Perry Mason, published nothing at all that year, having passed away in March at the age of eighty. Admittedly such old-timers as Rex Stout, Ngaio Marsh, Michael Innes and Gladys Mitchell were still playing the game with some of their old élan, but in truth their glory days had fallen behind them as well. Others, like Margery Allingham and John Street, had died within the last few years or, like Anthony Gilbert, Nicholas Blake, Leo Bruce and Christopher Bush, soon would expire or become debilitated. Decidedly in 1970—a year which saw the trials of the Manson family and the Chicago Seven, assorted bombings, kidnappings and plane hijackings by such terroristic entities as the Weathermen, the Red Army, the PLO and the FLQ, the American invasion of Cambodia and the Kent State shootings and the drug overdose deaths of Jimi Hendrix and Janis Joplin—leisure readers now more than ever stood in need of the intelligent escapism which classic crime fiction provided. Yet the old order in crime fiction, like that in world politics and society, seemed irrevocably to be washing away in a bloody tide of violent anarchy and all round uncouthness.

Or was it? Old values have a way of persisting. Even as the generation which produced the glorious detective fiction of the Golden Age finally began exiting the crime scene, a new generation of younger puzzle adepts had arisen, not to take the esteemed places of their elders, but to contribute their own worthy efforts to the rarefied field of fair play murder. Among these writers were P.D. James, Ruth Rendell, Emma Lathen, Patricia Moyes, H.R.F. Keating, Catherine Aird, Joyce Porter, Margaret Yorke, Elizabeth Lemarchand, Reginald Hill, Peter Lovesey and the author whom you are perusing now, Anne Morice (1916-1989). Morice, who like Yorke, Lovesey and Hill debuted as a mystery writer in 1970, was lavishly welcomed by critics in the United Kingdom (she was not published in the United States until 1974) upon the publication of her first mystery, *Death in the Grand Manor*, which suggestively and anachronistically was subtitled not an "extravaganza," but a novel of detection. Fittingly the book was lauded by no less than seemingly permanently retired Golden Age stalwarts Edmund Crispin and Francis Iles (aka Anthony Berkeley Cox). Crispin deemed Morice's debut puzzler "a charming whodunit . . . full of unforced buoyance" and prescribed it as a "remedy for existentialist gloom," while Iles, who would pass away at the age of seventy-seven less than six months after penning his review, found the novel a "most attractive lightweight," adding enthusiastically: "[E]ntertainingly written, it provides a modern version of the classical type of detective story. I was much taken with the cheerful young narrator . . . and I think most readers will feel the same way. Warmly recommended." Similarly, Maurice Richardson, who, although not a crime writer, had reviewed crime fiction for decades at the *London Observer*, lavished praise upon Morice's maiden mystery: "Entrancingly fresh and lively whodunit. . . . Excellent dialogue. . . . Much superior to the average effort to lighten the detective story."

With such a critical sendoff, it is no surprise that Anne Morice's crime fiction took flight on the wings of its bracing mirth. Over the next two decades twenty-five Anne Morice mysteries were published (the last of them posthumously), at the rate of one or two year. Twenty-three of these concerned the investigations of Tessa Crichton, a charming young actress who always manages to cross paths with murder, while two, written at the end of her career, detail cases of Detective Superintendent "Tubby" Wiseman. In 1976 Morice along with Margaret Yorke was chosen to become a member of Britain's prestigious Detection Club, preceding Ruth Rendell by a year, while in the 1980s her books were included in Bantam's superlative paperback "Murder

Most British" series, which included luminaries from both present and past like Rendell, Yorke, Margery Allingham, Patricia Wentworth, Christianna Brand, Elizabeth Ferrars, Catherine Aird, Margaret Erskine, Marian Babson, Dorothy Simpson, June Thomson and last, but most certainly not least, the Queen of Crime herself, Agatha Christie. In 1974, when Morice's fifth Tessa Crichton detective novel, *Death of a Dutiful Daughter*, was picked up in the United States, the author's work again was received with acclaim, with reviewers emphasizing the author's cozy traditionalism (though the term "cozy" had not then come into common use in reference to traditional English and American mysteries). In his notice of Morice's *Death of a Wedding Guest* (1976), "Newgate Callendar" (aka classical music critic Harold C. Schoenberg), Seventies crime fiction reviewer for the *New York Times Book Review*, observed that "Morice is a traditionalist, and she has no surprises [in terms of subject matter] in her latest book. What she does have, as always, is a bright and amusing style . . . [and] a general air of sophisticated writing." Perhaps a couple of reviews from Middle America—where intense Anglophilia, the dogmatic pronouncements of Raymond Chandler and Edmund Wilson notwithstanding, still ran rampant among mystery readers—best indicate the cozy criminal appeal of Anne Morice:

> Anne Morice . . . acquired me as a fan when I read her "Death and the Dutiful Daughter." In this new novel, she did not disappoint me. The same appealing female detective, Tessa Crichton, solves the mysteries on her own, which is surpris-

ing in view of the fact that Tessa is actually not a detective, but a film actress. Tessa just seems to be at places where a murder occurs, and at the most unlikely places at that . . . this time at a garden fete on the estate of a millionaire tycoon. . . . The plot is well constructed; I must confess that I, like the police, had my suspect all picked out too. I was "dead" wrong (if you will excuse the expression) because my suspect was also murdered before not too many pages turned. . . . This is not a blood-curdling, chilling mystery; it is amusing and light, but Miss Morice writes in a polished and intelligent manner, providing pleasure and entertainment. (Rose Levine Isaacson, review of *Death of a Heavenly Twin*, *Jackson Mississippi Clarion-Ledger*, 18 August 1974)

I like English mysteries because the victims are always rotten people who deserve to die. Anne Morice, like Ngaio Marsh et al., writes tongue in cheek but with great care. It is always a joy to read English at its glorious best. (Sally Edwards, "Ever-So British, This Tale," review of *Killing with Kindness*, *Charlotte North Carolina Observer*, 10 April 1975)

While it is true that Anne Morice's mysteries most frequently take place at country villages and estates, surely the quintessence of modern cozy mystery settings, there is a pleasing tartness to Tessa's narration and the brittle, epigrammatic dialogue which reminds me of the Golden Age Crime Queens (particularly Ngaio Marsh) and, to part from mystery for a moment, English playwright Noel Coward. Morice's books may be cozy but they most certainly are not cloying, nor are the sentiments which the characters express invariably "traditional." The author avoids any traces of soppiness or sentimentality and has a knack for clever turns of phrase which is characteristic of the bright young things of the Twenties and Thirties, the decades of her own youth. "Sackcloth and ashes would have been overdressing for the mood I had sunk into by then," Tessa reflects at one point in the novel *Death in the Grand Manor*. Never fear, however: nothing, not even the odd murder or two, keeps Tessa down in the dumps for long; and invariably she finds herself back on the trail of murder most foul, to the consternation of her handsome, debonair husband, Inspector Robin Price of Scotland Yard (whom she meets in the first novel in the series and has married by the second), and the exasperation of her amusingly eccentric and indolent playwright cousin, Toby Crichton, both of whom feature in almost all of the Tessa Crichton novels. Murder may not lastingly mar Tessa's equanimity, but she certainly takes her detection seriously.

Three decades now having passed since Anne Morice's crime novels were in print, fans of British mystery in both its classic and cozy forms should derive much pleasure in discovering (or rediscovering) her work in these new Dean Street Press editions and thereby passing time once again in that pleasant fictional English world where death affords us not emotional disturbance and distress but enjoyable and intelligent diversion.

Curtis Evans

CHAPTER ONE

ARRIVING home just before noon one scorching day last July after an hour-long, live broadcasting session, I had been prodding myself into the last little spurt with promises of ten minutes under a cool shower at the end of it and was scarcely half way to my goal when the front door bell rang.

At first glance the young woman on the doorstep was a stranger to me, though her own mother might have had trouble in recognising her, for she wore a black scarf over her head, completely obscuring her hair, and huge black sunglasses which she did not remove even when she had identified herself and been invited to step inside.

Her name was Brenda Parsons and although I had only met her on a single, and singularly distressing occasion, I had been friendly with her husband, Mike Parsons, for several years. He was a sound recordist, permanently employed by Associated International Productions, at whose studios near Wentworth I had worked in a number of films, and in addition to being consistently helpful and patient in the professional sense he had once gone out of his way to do me an enormous personal kindness.

It had happened right at the start of our acquaintance, on a cold and drizzly evening when I was embarking on the long trek home after a particularly arduous and frustrating day on the set. Within three minutes of turning out of the gates and heading the car towards London the engine had developed an alarming cough. After a few half-hearted attempts to control itself it gave up altogether and gently expired, only a quarter of a mile from base. Not being much of a hand at mechanics, I sat there for a while, cursing and whimpering and trying to summon the willpower to trudge back through the rain to the porter's lodge to telephone for help, when Mike Parsons drove past. He saw me and pulled into the side of the road, then backed his car up to mine.

I explained the predicament and, ignoring my protests, he spent about twenty minutes with his head under the bonnet, getting his hands black with grease and his legs soaking wet. He eventually tracked down the cause of the trouble, which I have now forgotten, but as the remedy depended on getting some new part or other, he offered to drive me to the nearest garage.

Nor was this all. Having explained matters there and arranged for my car to be towed in, he then insisted on delivering me to my own front door.

Several times during the journey I expressed my gratitude, but it was not until we reached Beacon Square that the true scale of his Samaritanism was brought home to me. I had invited him in for a drink, which he declined, explaining almost apologetically that he still had over an hour's drive ahead of him. It then transpired that he did not live in London at all but on a new housing estate near Reading and that he had driven at least thirty miles out of his way to do me this good turn.

Naturally we had remained on cordial terms ever since and, like numerous other people, I was always delighted when his name figured on the production unit, but we never met outside the studios. Despite his popularity, he was shy and retiring and, apart from his job, his whole life seemed to revolve round his wife, whom he referred to as Brennie, and their two little boys.

Once or twice since then I had caught him watching me with a rather wistful expression, but I could not even get him to join me in a drink at the commissariat. He told me that he had made it a rule to give up all that kind of self-indulgence soon after he married, when all the spare cash had to be put towards a house, but my single encounter with his wife had suggested that there might be an extra reason for his abstinence.

This was at the previous year's Christmas Eve party at A.I.P. Studios and, as invariably does happen at these macabre festivities, most people were lashing rather heavily into the wines and spirits. I confess that it had not occurred to me that Mrs Parsons was one of the ringleaders of this contingent. She was a flat-chested, mousey little female, very prim and dim, whom I had been introduced to soon after she arrived, and during our brief conversation she had struck me as being nervous and out of her element, fumbling for her words and not making much sense out of those which occurred to her, but there was nothing specially remarkable in that and I could well have been creating pretty much the same impression on her. So it came as a shock of staggering proportions when a little later on I saw her lurch against the buffet table and then, with no sound at all, pitch forward head first into the punch bowl, scattering canapés and glasses in all directions, from which predicament she was rescued in a detached and unemotional fashion by Mike, who carried her out, apparently unconscious.

The whole episode had been played out in only a couple of minutes, but it took the onlookers longer than that to recover. A blight descended on the party and people stood about looking shocked, embarrassed or amused, according to their natures, but none of us could pretend to be unaware of what had occurred. Just before the incident I had been talking to the studio manager, a somewhat sanctimonious individual named Alec Ferguson who had retained, or possibly cultivated, a strong Glaswegian accent and suitably pawky manner to match, and I asked him what could possibly have caused it.

"Now, now, dear, don't come the innocent! Anyone could see she'd had a wee drop too much," he replied, making a tilting gesture with his glass, lest his meaning escape me.

"Well yes," I admitted, "I agree that's the simple answer, but I don't understand how anyone could have got so drunk so fast. They'd only been here for about twenty minutes. Perhaps she was genuinely ill? Do you think someone ought to go and find out? It could be serious."

"Oh, it's serious all right, make no mistake," Alec informed me loftily. "And I respect your charitable construction of the matter, but the truth is more likely that she was stoned when she got here. Poor old Mike!" he added with a lachrymose sigh.

"You mean this kind of thing has happened before?"

"Oh aye, she's quite celebrated for it. Had you not heard?"

"No, but I never met her until this evening."

"And that's no surprise either. The poor laddie usually manages to keep her out of temptation's way, but she certainly made up for her lost ground tonight. It's a terrible thing for a decent chap like him to be saddled with such a burden."

*

Recalling this conversation as Brenda and I confronted each other in the hall, I was disturbed to see that her hands were trembling violently, obliging her to place her bag on the table, and the fact that she had not removed her sunglasses was also open to a rather depressing interpretation. However, social custom dies hard and when she had stammered out a request that I should spare her a few minutes and we had moved into the drawing room, I found myself automatically offering her a drink.

To my surprise and relief, she refused, adding not over-graciously that she could do with a cup of tea if it wouldn't be any trouble. It was quite a lot of trouble as it happened because Mrs Cheeseman, who works for us when she is able to, is very inventive about finding new hiding places and I spent a tedious ten minutes tracking down the tea caddy. Also I resented every second's delay in finding out why Brenda had come at all. When the full story came out I was inclined to attribute her visit to the circumstance of my husband's being a police detective, although she maintained right up to the end that it was my personal advice she was seeking.

I eventually returned with the tray and placed it beside her and then drew one pair of curtains, blocking out most of the light, on the pretext of making the room a little cooler. I doubt if it did so, but it certainly had the desired effect of forcing her to take off her glasses in order to distinguish between the cup and the sugar bowl. Having done so, she turned her head away from me, though not fast enough to prevent my seeing her puffy pink lids. The sight of them instantly made me feel guilty, for I realised that the glasses had masked either some eye infection or the fact that she had been crying for hours on end.

"What's the trouble?" I asked, trying to adopt a bracing tone. "Something wrong with Mike?"

She nodded, pressing a handkerchief to her mouth and then, to my utter astonishment, she asked:

"You wouldn't have seen him, by any chance?"

"Not lately, no. I regret to say that I haven't set foot in a film studio for over a month."

"I didn't mean there. The studio people don't know where he is either. I just thought you might possibly have heard from him? He hasn't many friends outside his work and I don't know who else to ask."

I stared at her: "You mean you really have no idea where he is?"

She shook her head, dumbly at first, then after a sip of tea said in a stronger voice:

"That's about it and it's driving me round the bend. I know I've no right to lumber you with my troubles, but I happened to hear you on the radio this morning and you sounded so sort of warm and friendly, if you know what I mean, so I thought, 'Here goes!' Besides, I remembered you'd been kind to me at that god-awful party. I was scared silly and you were about the only person who bothered to come near me. I was hoping you might be able to help me now."

"And so I will, if I can, but why were you scared silly?"

"I'm not sure really, but I was feeling awful that evening. Can't understand what came over me, but the fact is that I've never been any use at parties at the best of times. Can't communicate, I suppose. I'm hopeless with strangers and film people are the worst of all. It's such a closed shop and I always feel they're despising me. Mike never likes to talk about his work when he's at home and he doesn't invite any of his mates to the house, so it's not all my fault that I can't get on with them. Just the same, I always feel such a nit. I still don't understand what came over me that evening though. Don't remember much about it, to be honest with you."

"And there hasn't been any more recent occasion where the same kind of thing happened? What I mean is, something which you don't remember too well, but which upset Mike and caused him to go off on his own for a bit?"

"No, honestly, Miss Crichton, there's been nothing like that, I swear. Everything was perfectly normal right up to the minute he left. That's what makes me feel so awful. It's not knowing what's made him do it and whether he means to come back which has got me into such a state."

"Yes, I can understand that, but isn't there somebody closer to you that you could confide in? Someone in your family, for instance?"

"No, I've only got my sister. She lives up North, and a fat lot she cares!"

"What about neighbours?"

"Oh no, I couldn't say anything to them, I'd rather die. They're such a snoopy lot, most of them, and they'd simply lap up a story like this. Besides, they'd talk about it in front of their children and then it would get back to Barry and Keith. Those are our two boys. I'm trying to keep it from them for as long as I can. I've told them their Dad is doing a job on location. He often doesn't get home until after they're in bed and sometimes he has to work weekends and that, but all the same I think they sense there's something wrong. For one thing, Mike usually manages to phone me when he has to spend a night away."

"Who's looking after the boys today?"

"Oh, they're both at school now. Barry's seven and Keith started this term, he's just five. They stay for school dinner, so I don't have to meet them till four. That's when they'll begin asking about their Daddy and I'll have to invent some more lies for them. Honestly, I don't think I can go on much longer. That's why I've come to you. You struck me as a bit more human than most of the gang he works with. And then again you were one of the few people he used to talk about when he was at home. I thought he might possibly have been in touch with you."

I shook my head. "Sorry, no. We aren't really on those terms, you know."

"Yes, I suppose it was a silly idea really. Mike never was one for giving much of himself away. Not even to me. Isn't it awful to think you can share a bed with someone for nearly ten years and still know so little about them that when they walk out on you you haven't a clue about where they might have gone to? No, if I'm honest, I suppose the real reason I came here was that I was afraid I'd go mad if I didn't talk to someone and I was hoping you'd at least listen and give me some advice."

"I'm sorry," I said again. "I'd love to help you, I really would. I'm fond of Mike and it doesn't sound at all in character for him to behave like this, but I'm afraid the only advice I can give you is to go straight to the police."

"Oh no, I couldn't do that," she replied at once, and more or less as I had anticipated.

"Why not? They can be very discreet."

"Oh, I daresay, but all the same they'd come round asking questions of all the neighbours and everything. It stands to reason, doesn't it? And I couldn't bear that.

Besides, Mike would be livid if he found out. He must have had some reason for going off like he has and if . . . when he comes back he'd be furious with me for making it public property. He can't stand people poking into his affairs."

"But listen, Mrs Parsons . . ."

"Oh, do call me Brenda."

"All right, and my name is Tessa by the way. What I was going to say, Brenda, was that you may have got it all wrong. Perhaps he's been in a car accident and is suffering from loss of memory? It can happen, you know. He might be sitting in some police station at this very moment, while they check through the list of missing persons."

She looked at me doubtfully. "Yes, I've thought of that, naturally, but it's just not on. For one thing, he always carries a cartload of stuff around in his pocket book. You know, driving licence, credit card, all that lot. And he's taken his wallet with him, I'm certain of that. I've searched everywhere and it's not in the house. He was driving his own car too, so if he's been injured in a road accident they could still have traced him through the registration number."

"So he's taken the car, has he? Doesn't that put you in rather a fix?"

"No, I don't drive, you see. Tried to learn once or twice, but I couldn't seem to get the hang of it. Mike said my reflexes were too slow or something. Anyway, the car wouldn't be much use to me because he always takes it to drive to work. There isn't any other way for him to get there."

"And what else did he take, if you don't mind my asking? Clothes? Razor? Things like that?"

She hesitated, picking up the sunglasses and twiddling them around in her hand, as though tempted to put them on again and I said hastily:

"Forgive me, that was a foolish question. I know that if someone asked me the same thing about Robin I wouldn't have the faintest idea how many shirts and pullovers he possesses, or razors either, come to that."

She sighed: "Well, you've got more excuse, I suppose. I mean, being an actress and having your own career and everything."

"I don't feel the need of an excuse," I told her. "No one would expect Robin to know how many shoes and hats I have."

"Well, that's different, isn't it? I mean, a wife is expected to take care of her husband's belongings. At least, that's how most people see it, but they shouldn't set themselves up to judge really. Mike's very self-reliant, you know. Always buys his own clothes and takes them to the cleaners himself and all that."

"Yes, and perhaps he's not so exceptional as you imagine. To get back to the main problem, though, what makes you so convinced that this isn't a case of amnesia? I don't want to add to your worries, but supposing he'd been mugged and knocked unconscious and had his wallet stolen?"

"The trouble is, people don't get mugged lying in bed in their own house, do they?"

"Well, that's probably true," I admitted, "but I'm not sure if I follow you."

She nodded: "I know, I explain things badly. Look, Tessa, if it's not an awful bind for you, could I tell you from the beginning? Even talking this much has made me feel calmer and you never know, you might notice some point I'd missed when you've heard the lot."

I made no claims to altruism in giving my consent, for I was bursting with curiosity, but another sort of appetite was also forcing itself on my attention and I said:

"Okay, but let's first of all go into the kitchen and find something to eat. Personally, I'm starving and you don't look as though you've had a square meal lately. You can talk to me while I'm getting it ready."

CHAPTER TWO

OMITTING most of the repetitions as well as my own queries and interruptions and putting it all into a straight sequence, Brenda's story was as follows:

"It began on Monday night," she said. "That would be three days ago now. Mike got home about nine, after the kids were asleep. Yes, it was a bit late. He'd been doing a lot of overtime lately, including the Saturday and Sunday. It was some American production they were recording over here, as far as I can remember. Anyway, they'd finished it all up on the Monday and he and the rest of the sound crew had been given Tuesday off.

"Yes, he was a bit on the tired side, but nothing out of the ordinary. He looks frail, but he's very strong and wiry, you know, and he's accustomed to long hours. They often have these spurts when they want to finish on schedule and don't have to worry about costs. He was in a cheerful mood too, looking forward to getting a few jobs done in the garden and if the weather held we were going to have a look at some boats. We've only got a small thing at the moment, with an outboard motor, but now the boys are getting bigger Mike thought they'd be able to handle something more ambitious, and it's always been his dream to own a really swanky job. He'd marked one or two possibles in the local paper and he was going to ring round in the morning and fix up for us all to go and see them after school. Looking back on it, there doesn't seem to have been a hint of anything wrong that evening.

"No, he didn't want any supper. He'd managed to get a sandwich in the canteen during a break and he never drinks, as you probably know. So we both had some cocoa and talked for a bit; about an hour all told, I suppose it was, and then we went to bed.

"The next morning, Tuesday that would be, I got up at my usual time, which is seven, but Mike was still asleep and I moved around very quietly so as not to disturb him. I warned the boys about it too. They're good kids, not like some of the hooligans on our estate, and they did their best not to make a sound. I kept the kitchen door shut while we had our breakfast and when I'd stacked every-thing into the dishwasher we went off to school.

"No, I don't have to take them the whole way, only as far as the school bus, which goes from the new shop-ping centre at the bottom of the hill. It's about half a mile down from where we live. Mike sometimes drops them off at the school on his way to the studios, but mostly I take them to the bus and I always meet them off it just after four. Well, yes, they could easily walk up on their own, but as I've said, there's rather a rough crowd on our estate and we don't want Barry and Keith mixing with them more than we can help.

"It must have been getting on for half past nine by the time I got home again that morning. The bus left at twenty to, but I wanted to do some shopping while I was down there and I had to wait around for the supermarket to open. I hadn't been expecting Mike home for lunch, you see, and I was right out of everything. I thought I might as well make some Cornish pasties, which are one of his favourites, so I needed a bit of steak and some flour and one or two other things. Took me about half an hour, all told.

"There wasn't a sign of Mike when I got in, so I set to and made the pastry and put it aside in the refrigerator. Then I went upstairs and tidied the boys' bedroom. That brought it to after ten o'clock and the door of our room was still tight shut, but Mike doesn't sleep as late as that as a rule, and I thought he might be lying there, hoping I'd bring him a cup of tea. So I opened the door very gently and peeped inside. That's when I got my first shock because he wasn't there.

"No, I can't exactly explain why it scared me. It was just a lot of small things. For example, he'd stripped the bed back to air, and folded his pyjamas and hung up his dressing gown and that struck me as a bit odd. It's such a treat for him not to have to go haring off to the studios first thing in the morning that when he does get the chance he likes to spoil himself a bit. You know, saunter about the garden in his dressing gown, pulling off the dead heads, little things like that, and then spending ages in the bathroom as likely as not. But he wasn't in the bathroom, and another thing that struck me as funny was the way he'd closed the bedroom door behind him when he came out. I don't think people normally do that, do they? It was almost as though he'd wanted me to believe he was still in there, though I couldn't for the life of me see why.

"Well, scared is too strong a word really. More puzzled and a bit put out is how you could describe it. But anyway it wasn't much later when I was able to tell myself how silly I'd been to get upset. I'd started to make the bed and I happened to look out of the window, which was when I saw that one end of the hedge which separates our garden from the field was all neat and tidy and the wheelbarrow beside it piled up with branches and clippings. You haven't ever been to our house, but it's the end one on the estate and we've got a bigger garden than the rest of them. From where I was looking you can't see any other buildings at all. Just this big field, with those black and white cows in it, and then the woods, which go right down almost as far as the river. It's a lovely spot and we were lucky to get it really, especially at the price we did, but this hedge has always been a bugbear. We can't do away with it because of the cows getting in and trampling all over the garden, but it seems to grow so fast and it gets on my nerves to see it all straggly. I'm always on at Mike about trimming it back.

"Well anyway, when I saw he'd made a start on it I felt a bit ashamed of myself. 'So he was playing a trick on me, after all,' I thought. 'Only it was meant to be a nice surprise. I was to think he was upstairs having a lie in, and then he'd stroll indoors and tell me to take a look out of the window.'

"The trouble with *that* was that he didn't come indoors. I'd finished off one or two more jobs in the house and there wasn't much needed doing by then, so I put the kettle on and went out to the garden, meaning to call him in to come and have some coffee. I was practising how I'd do it, you know, pretend I hadn't known what he was up to and being ever so chuffed about the hedge and everything, but it was all wasted because he wasn't in the garden at all.

"No, I didn't exactly panic, even then. It was more of a sort of empty, let-down feeling, if you can follow me. The hedge was only about half done and the shears were lying on the ground beside the wheelbarrow. He never leaves off a job without putting everything away after him, so I worked it out that he must have downed tools to run up and answer the phone. We've put in an outside bell, on the patio, so he'd have heard it from where he was standing. It might have been some crisis at the studio they were ringing him about, and if so he would quite likely have dropped everything and dashed off there. I thought he'd probably ring me as soon as he got the chance, and I decided to go ahead and make the pasties anyway and we'd at least be able to have them for supper. But first of all I went out to the garage to see if the car had gone and it had, so that more or less settled it.

"No, I couldn't have seen earlier that the garage was empty. For one thing, me not being a driver, cars don't mean so much to me as they seem to most people, and another thing is that we always keep the garage locked, whether the car's there or not. We store a lot of things in there, you see, like fishing tackle and the rubber dinghy. At least, we did when we had one. Barry got larking about with it the other day and it capsized; but there's several other things too, and we always load up with sticks and kindling when we go picnicking in the woods and that.

We have a lot of trouble in that way with some of the neighbouring kids. There's one family who wouldn't hesitate to help themselves as soon as our backs were turned. Mike complained about it to the parents once or twice, but they didn't want to know, so the only thing was to lock up every time.

"Well, I thought that too. I did think it was a bit strange he hadn't left me a note, and that was the very next thing I did; started looking round for one, suddenly struck me that if he'd gone out at about nine o'clock, which he must have when you think of it, he'd have felt certain of meeting me on my way up from the bus and that would have given him the chance to explain. You have to pass through the shopping area to get on to the main road, so that's exactly what would have happened, if only I hadn't taken it into my head to spend all that time at the supermarket.

"Well, that's how my mind was working then, mind you, but it isn't any longer. Except for going down again to meet the boys at four o'clock, I stayed indoors the whole day, so as to be near the phone, but there was only one call. It did come from the studios, as far as I could make out, only it wasn't Mike, it was somebody wanting to speak to him. Around eleven, that must have been. It was funny really because he didn't give his full name, just said, 'This is Sandy speaking', and then when I said Mike wasn't in he rang off before I could say another word.

"Well no, now you mention it, I couldn't swear he was anything to do with A.I.P., only the call came through a switchboard operator, so I just took it for granted. I don't know where else he could have been calling from.

"It's funny you should ask that because he did have some sort of accent. American, it sounded like. Anyway, after that there was only one other thing to break the monotony and that was when the man came to read the electric meter. That was the worst moment of all, in a funny way, because he came in one of those greyish sort of vans they use and it was almost the same size and colour as our old estate car. When I caught sight of it I thought for a moment that Mike had come back and I was just starting to tell myself what an old silly I'd been when I saw this man in uniform walking up the drive. I felt so awful then that I think I began to cry. I couldn't even tell him where the meter was and, poor man, he hadn't been to us before. He must have thought I was dotty or something. Still, I pulled myself together in the end and after that the day just sort of dragged on until it was time to meet the boys. They had their supper at the usual time and I made up some yarn about their Daddy having to fill in unexpectedly for someone on location and that he'd probably be back tomorrow or the next day, and then we'd be able to do all the things he'd promised us, but I could see that at the back of their minds they didn't really believe me. No, they didn't argue exactly, but they just kept changing the subject every time I mentioned it. It gave me the weirdest sensation, like trying to push a needle through a brick wall. It got so bad that after I'd put them to bed I had to go out to look at the hedge to convince myself that I hadn't dreamt it all. It was quite a relief to find the wheelbarrow and shears still there and everything just as I'd remembered it.

"Well yes, I suppose I can account for it, if I'm honest with you. For one thing, they'd been asleep when he got home the night before, so they didn't get a glimpse of him on Tuesday morning, but there was more to it than that. To tell you the truth, Tessa, I had a kind of breakdown a year or two back. Nothing serious, but I kept getting these migraines and dizzy spells and so on. I know Mike did his best to make them understand that it was only a passing thing, but you can never tell with kids, can you? I'm sure he meant well but I think they got it into their heads I was half cracked or something.

"Well, let's see, where was I? Yes, that's right, Tuesday evening. Still no word from Mike and I was so worried I didn't go to bed at all that night. I didn't see how I could and leave the door unlocked and I wasn't even sure that Mike had taken his key. So I sat up and watched the T.V. until it closed down, though I couldn't tell you the first thing about any of the programmes I saw, and then I dozed off on the sofa for an hour or two. Luckily, it gets light very early this time of year and I got up about five and made myself some tea and did a bit of cleaning up to take my mind off things, and then after I'd taken the boys down to the bus I plucked up courage to ring the studios.

"No, it wasn't so much that he minds me phoning him there, though he's not too keen on it, as it happens. The reason I'd put off doing it before was that it would be like throwing away my last hope. I suppose I knew in my heart of hearts that he wouldn't be there, and then I'd really have to face up to the fact that he'd walked out on us, without even a word of explanation.

"Anyway, I didn't ask for him personally. I spoke to the Studio Manager, Mr Ferguson. Hateful beast he is, too. And he didn't know a thing. I felt like putting the receiver down as soon as I heard that, but I had to listen to him going on and on, pretending to be very worried about Mike, although you could tell he was revelling in it. There's something so mean and spiteful about him and I bet the story was all round the studios in five minutes. They'll all have been laughing their heads off about it.

"No, I suppose it doesn't really matter, but Mike won't be very pleased about it when he goes in to work next week, as I think he's bound to. Even if he's walked out on me and the boys he'll still have his living to earn and you know as well as I do that jobs, steady ones at any rate, aren't all that easy to come by in the film business. That's mainly why I didn't go to the police. I thought I'd done him enough damage already by phoning the studios. If you tell me there's no other way, then I suppose I'll have to bring them into it, but I do wish there was just one thing I could try first. Mike was always telling me how clever you were and I thought you might have some ideas."

It goes without saying that this final appeal put me on my mettle and I said:

"Perhaps I can offer you a compromise. If you don't mind, I'd like to talk to Robin about it. He'll be home for dinner and I could sound him out. On a purely personal level, naturally. It needn't go any further and at the very least he'll know whether there's anything constructive your local police could do at this stage. If not, then nothing has been lost. If he thinks there might be, then it will be up to you to decide. Is that a deal?"

"Oh, all right, if that's the best you can think of," she said sullenly, then took herself in hand and looking up at me smiled bleakly.

"Excuse me, Tessa, I didn't mean to be rude. It's all got so much on top of me that I don't know what I'm saying half the time. It's very good of you to bother, and I do appreciate it, truly I do. Just telling you about it has done me good. I'd better go now, though, or I'll miss the two-fifty and it wouldn't do for the boys to come back to an empty house. Could I give you a ring in the morning, when you've talked to your husband?"

"No, it might be better if I were to call you. I'm not quite sure what time I'll be going out. Let me write down your number."

It was quite inexplicable, but this simple request seemed to undo everything that had been built up. Brenda's mouth sagged open and she stared at me for a moment in petrified silence, then pushed aside the plate of half-eaten scrambled eggs, sank her head down on her arms and began to sob.

Thoroughly mystified, I let her get on with it for a while and busied myself at the telephone. When I turned round again the crying was over and she was putting on her sunglasses.

"They'll be here in ten minutes," I told her.

"There was no need to order a cab. I could have gone by bus."

"Not if you're to be at Paddington in time for the two-fifty. And please don't worry about the fare because they'll put it on my account. After all, it's entirely my fault that you've been delayed. If only I'd known where Mrs Cheeseman kept the eggs this emergency wouldn't have arisen."

"Well, thanks, then. It's ever so kind of you. I am a bit short, as it happens, but I'll let you have it back as soon as I get myself sorted out."

"You're not in serious difficulties about money, are you? If so, how about a loan to tide you over for a few days?"

"No, I'll be all right, thanks. Mike and I have a joint account and there must have been quite a lot paid in last week, with all the overtime. The trouble is I haven't been able to get down to the bank. I haven't liked to leave the house more than I could help, in case he should try and ring. But that's silly, I can see it now. If he does want to get in touch with me he knows better than anyone when to catch me at home. I'll cash a cheque tomorrow as soon as they open."

"So about getting in touch with you tomorrow?" I said hesitantly as we waited outside for her mini-cab, trusting to luck that she would not instantly collapse in a heap on the pavement. "What's the best way to organise it?"

"Oh yes, you ring me," she replied firmly. "I'm sorry for going to pieces like that when you suggested it; but you see it hardly ever rings when he's not there, so now if I do hear the bell I think it must be him and I get so worked up I can hardly bring myself to answer it. But that's silly too and I've got to get over it. Just tell me what time it's likely to be and then I'll know it's you and be able to cope."

"Shall we say lunch time, then?" I suggested as the cab drew up beside us. "As near one o'clock as I can make it. And cheer up, Brenda! I'm sure there'll have been some news by then."

With the black opaque lenses masking her expression, I could not tell whether these conventional phrases brought her any comfort or not, but curiously enough they turned out to be perfectly true.

CHAPTER THREE

"So, PLENTY of situation and character building," I concluded, when reporting to Robin. "But so far not much plot development."

"No," he agreed. "And I must warn you that the plot, such as it is, is all too predictable."

"Why so?"

"Well, the details vary from case to case, naturally, but in essence the story is no different from a thousand others."

"Really? You mean that lots of people suddenly vanish for no reason?"

"Oh, there's generally a reason, but that's more or less what I mean, yes. Of course the vast majority are teenagers casting off the parental shackles, but it happens with husbands and wives too."

"And are the husbands and wives usually traced?"

"No, very rarely. Just occasionally it's a genuine case of amnesia or nervous breakdown and so on, which gets itself sorted out, but in the main they're never seen again and no one ever discovers what became of them, or why they went. And that's another thing; it may look like a sudden impulse, but to cover one's tracks so successfully must need a certain amount of advance planning."

"And you think that Mike Parsons is one of those?"

"Shouldn't wonder," Robin said, glancing sideways at the evening paper. "Did he take his passport?"

"I never thought of asking."

"I'm afraid you'll never make a detective, Tessa."

"Oh yes, I will," I retorted. "Not in your class, maybe, but one shouldn't overlook the psychological aspects."

He did not seem impressed. "Shouldn't one?" he asked drawing the paper nearer to him.

"And they sometimes bring results."

"Good! So you won't be needing any help from me?"

"Yes, I will, and do stop trying to sneak a look at that newspaper. I have promised to tell Brenda freely and frankly whether you think there is anything to be gained by reporting it to the police."

"Freely and frankly, no I don't."

"Why not?"

"Because so far as we know he hasn't committed any crime and there's nothing to stop him going wherever he chooses. You may despise my prosaic methods, but I think you'll find that he either turns up in a couple of days with the hangover of the century, or else that he has taken his passport. In which case, he could be in Brazil by now. I can't see anything to prevent his getting in touch with his wife if he wants to, so the chances are that he doesn't and has gone to considerable lengths to keep her in the dark. If she can't offer a clue to his whereabouts, I don't see how you can expect the police to."

"I don't despise your prosaic methods at all. I just maintain that on their own they're not always enough. Mike is an angel of kindness and no amount of statistics will make me believe that he could behave in such a cruel and callous way."

"Ah ha! Here we go again!"

"Go where again?"

"How often have I heard words like those? More than I could count. 'But she was such a sweet obedient girl', 'No, he didn't seem depressed in any way', 'Oh yes, a most devoted husband, never complained'. That's the kind of thing they all say every time. The sad truth is, Tessa, that nobody ever really knows the full story about another human being, not even husbands and wives."

"That's exactly what Brenda said. It depressed me at the time and it's depressing me again now; but if you're right why did he bother to come home at all on Monday night? Why not just have left for work in the morning and not returned? He'd been doing a lot of overtime lately, so she wouldn't have been seriously worried until about midnight. It would have given him a good clear start."

"I can think of several reasons, one being that he may not have made up his mind to bolt until Monday night. Perhaps he arrived home tired and hungry and looking forward to a few home comforts and found her dead drunk on the sofa. It could well have been the breaking point which made him feel he simply couldn't take any more."

"And leave his two children at the mercy of a confirmed alcoholic? That doesn't sound like Mi—Oh, very well, but in that case, it wasn't a planned escape after all? Just this sudden impulse?"

"He had all night to work on it, don't forget. And it could have been quite a night if it began with his carting her up to bed in a drunken stupor."

I considered this view of the matter for a while and then said: "Somehow, I don't see it, Robin. I know from first hand experience that she has her bouts, although she covers them up with genteel euphemisms like 'migraines' and 'dizzy spells', but I doubt if there have been any recently. If ever a woman had an excuse for hitting the bottle now it's her and yet I couldn't get her to drink anything except a cup of tea."

"You can't tell. The shock may have sobered her up temporarily, but apart from that she didn't necessarily have to be plastered when he arrived home. Supposing she'd pitched in by nagging him about the damned hedge or something? From your description she sounds quite a little whiner."

"Yes, and probably neurotically houseproud too, with a strong dash of persecution mania thrown in. In times of stress her only recourse seems to be to plunge into another round of scrubbing and polishing, but you'd think Mike would be used to that by now. After all, they've been married for ten years and he's the man who skips off home as soon as the whistle blows. In fact, I'd have said he was quite as much the little homebody as Brenda, which makes the whole thing so extremely puzzling."

"Well, you've met him and I haven't, so I'll have to take your word for that, but perhaps you'd care to hear another suggestion as to why he came home on Monday evening?"

"Yes, very much."

"Simply that he was forced to because when he left in the morning he forgot one vital piece of equipment; like, let us say, his passport."

"You seem to set great store by this passport?"

"Yes, because it may be crucial in establishing whether he went off of his own free will, or under some compulsion, particularly if . . ."

"If what?"

"You'll probably howl me down and say it's psychologically inadmissible and all the rest of it, but I was going to add: 'particularly if there's another woman involved'."

Since he had adequately expressed my protests for me there was nothing much left to say, but I was faintly piqued by his easy assumption that this was just one more case of a husband tiring of the domestic bonds and setting forth in search of pastures new, and by his still easier assumption that Brenda probably had only herself to blame. It was a slur, if ever I heard one, and apart from wanting a happy ending for the Parsons, I was keen as mustard to turn up some evidence to prove that in this instance at least Robin had misjudged the matter.

If he was secretly hoping for the opposite, we were possibly both about equally disappointed, for the ensuing twenty-four hours were to produce two fresh items, one of which strengthened his theory while the other knocked a couple of gaping holes in it.

"No passport," I announced on Friday evening.

"So he did take it with him? I won't pretend that I'm altogether surprised."

"Yes, you are, because I didn't mean that at all. I meant, literally, no passport. He's never had one."

"How strange! Are you sure?"

"According to Brenda, and she ought to know."

"But what about holidays abroad and all that?"

"They didn't have them. Apparently he got so little time off that his idea of bliss was holidays at home, clipping the hedges and taking his family on outings on the river. They did once all go on an excursion to Holland to see the tulips, but you don't need a real passport for that. Though speaking, mark you, from the purely psychological viewpoint, I'm willing to bet that he'd have taken his passport along with him on that occasion if he had possessed one."

"But I thought you film lot were forever shooting off to far flung corners of the world?"

"Not sound crews, funnily enough. At least, not Mike's variety. His job is dubbing and post synch, and that sort of thing. Strictly studio work."

"I see. However, it doesn't preclude the possibility of his having acquired a passport without his wife's knowledge."

"Just what I said to myself."

"What? No psychological barriers?"

"None. In fact, I thought we could resolve the point in a much more positive way. I am sure it would be easy for someone like yourself to check whether a passport has been issued in his name or not. If so, it was probably fairly recent, so it shouldn't take long."

"Well, I'm damned! So you're quite willing to make use of my clodhopping methods when it suits you?"

"More than willing. In fact, it's the combination of our two methods which ought to make us invincible. I'm even prepared to do a little clodhopping myself from time to time and I can provide you with just the sort of information you will approve of."

"How kind!"

"You see, I thought plain Michael Parsons might be too vague, specially if he'd applied in person and given a false address, so here it is in detail: Michael James Barry Parsons, and he was born in Auckland on 4th September, 1938."

"Thank you very much. Though why I should thank you for dragging me into your tiresome imbroglios I simply cannot imagine," Robin said, nevertheless making a note of the information. "And how did you come by all that, may I ask?"

"By telling the truth, naturally. Isn't that always your advice?"

"Try not to be smug, darling. And I suppose I shall be completely buried under your coals of fire if it turns out that he hasn't got a passport? I have to admit that it would alter the complexion of things. He surely couldn't be so innocent as to imagine he could hide out for long in this tight little island? In my experience, the harder people try to tuck themselves away in some remote corner the more likely they are to run slap into their next-door neighbour."

"Nevertheless, I have to tell you that this is what Brenda now believes he has done."

"Why's that?"

"There's been a fresh development and you'd better get ready to shovel your own coals of fire because it backs up your theory and lets mine down with a hollow thud. It came to light this morning when Brenda went to the bank. She wanted to draw twenty pounds in cash, but instead of handing it over in the normal way, the cashier gave her what she describes as 'a funny look'. It eventually transpired that the joint account had a balance of approximately thirty pence. All the rest had been drawn out by her husband a few days before he disappeared. Of course there wouldn't have been any real trouble about letting her have the twenty pounds, but the account had never been overdrawn before and he thought she ought to know how she stood."

"And how much should there have been in it?"

"Between two and three hundred pounds. Apparently, it normally stands at around that figure by the middle of the month. What happens is that Mike has all his salary paid into the account at the beginning of the month and part of it is regularly transferred to some kind of savings account. He pays all the quarterly bills and mortgage and so on and Brenda draws a regular weekly sum for the housekeeping and her own and the children's clothes. All very orderly and efficient."

"And when did he draw out this lump sum?"

"Last Thursday evening, on his way home from work. They have a late opening on Thursdays. He never breathed a word of it to Brenda though, and I must say it's changed her attitude completely. She's hopping mad, which is a good sign in a way, because she's now ready to tell all to the police."

"All the same, unless he's fixed himself up with some job overseas, two or three hundred quid is not going to take him very far. He'll have to get work somewhere and there aren't all that many film studios to choose from in this country."

"Don't I know it?" I said sadly. "But there's still the deposit account, you know. There's nothing joint about that and Brenda doesn't even know how much he has in it. Besides, it doesn't have to be films. He must know quite a lot about electronics and that sort of thing and I know for a fact that he's very clever with car engines."

"Which reminds me: what about the car?"

"It's an old grey estate car, she says."

"I don't mean that. I was thinking that if she does want the police to try and trace him the car will be their best lead. Will she be able to tell them the registration number?"

"Yes, she will."

"Then she must be a woman in a million. I bet you can't remember ours?"

"You're so right, but I don't happen to be the mother of Barry and Keith. Little boys always have that sort of thing at their finger tips. Not that I share your view that it will be much help. Flogging the car is probably the first thing he'll do. And the second, I daresay, will be to move on to another garage and get a new one for cash. For all we know, he may have opened a secret bank account in another part of the country. There's nothing illegal in that, is there?"

"No, and if that's what he has done, I still think it will turn out to be in some foreign country. However, there's nothing you nor I can do about it now."

"Does that mean you're not going to follow it up for me after all my hard clodhopping?"

"Not now you've told me she intends to report it herself. It'll be in the hands of the local branch now and I shouldn't dream of interfering. Good thing too, as it happens, because it may surprise you to learn that I have one or two affairs of my own which need urgent attention at present. All of which leads up to breaking the news that even though it is Saturday I have to work tomorrow, I'm afraid. Sorry about that, but I'll get back as early as I can."

"Though not in time for lunch?"

"Unlikely. Why?"

"Oh, nothing much. Simply that you appear to have forgotten that we're supposed to lunch with the Nicholsons tomorow."

"No, I hadn't. I thought you'd make my excuses and go on your own. You know them well enough for that, surely?"

"Perhaps I do and perhaps I don't. I'll have to decide in the morning. Will you need the car?"

"No, why?"

"Just checking."

"I can't believe you would bother to get the car out just for that. They only live two streets away."

"Yes, so they do."

"In fact, I should think it would take you as long to walk to the garage as to walk to the Nicholsons."

I didn't bother to comment on this, nor did I think there was a need to. Robin was giving me the sort of look which indicated clearly that he had a shrewd idea of what was passing through my mind and then, after a resigned shake of his head, he reached out a hand and promptly got stuck into his beloved evening paper.

CHAPTER FOUR

GUY Nicholson answered the telephone and informed me that Belinda was in the bath, which could not have been more satisfactory. Men are so blessedly incurious about these matters and he sounded almost relieved when I explained that Robin had to work and that I had received an unexpected rehearsal call; whereas Belinda would probably have gone on digging and probing until I was forced to invent all sorts of unnecessary lies and excuses.

Having struck lucky with my first blow I took good care to be out of the house before she could get the bath towel round her and as a result arrived at Number 32 Hill Grove well ahead of the appointed time.

Both the house and its surroundings were distinctly grander than imagination had led me to expect. I had visualised a closely packed arrangement of modest, red-brick houses, possibly in the neo-Georgian style, and indeed I passed a good many such before coming into reasonably open country, a mile or so up from the river. Hill Grove was literally a hill, rising up from a flat landscape of meadows and woods and the houses were of a more than ordinarily adventurous pattern, with a strong Scandinavian flavour. They were built of timber and were dotted around on different points of the hillside. A straggly lane connected the estate to a minor road at the foot, itself following a gentler descent to the main London road, which ran at right angles to it through the new shopping centre and from there to river level. Each house was detached and gained an added distinction from the fact that, due no doubt to the exigencies of the site, the distances between them varied considerably and they did not all face in the same direction.

Number 32, although the highest numerically, was at the opposite end in the geographical sense and thus the first to be reached from the lane. This fact also contributed to my early arrival, for I had anticipated all manner of difficulties and delays in locating the house, not one of which materialised, and the sight of two neatly dressed boys riding their shining immaculate bicycles round a shaven, immaculate lawn convinced me that I had reached my destination even before I came close enough to read the number on the gate.

Barry and Keith dismounted when they saw my car pull up and stood watching me as I fumbled with the latch of the wrought iron gate. Then, as it swung open, they both dropped their bicycles on the grass and the younger boy bolted round to the back of the house, while the other walked slowly towards me.

He was a round-faced, placid-looking child, with light brown hair cut straight across his forehead in a wide fringe, and small, regular features very like his father's. He did not appear at all shy and the wary, almost reluctant approach obviously did not spring from timidity, for when he was close enough he addressed me in confident, faintly reprimanding tones:

"Are you Miss Crichton?"

"Yes. And you're Barry? Or is it Keith?"

"Barry. Keith is my brother. You can bring your car in the drive, if you like. Actually, you ought not to leave it out there because some of the others come down rather fast and they might bash into it."

He evidently shared his parents' low opinion of the neighbours and, having no proof that it was unjustified, I obediently returned to the car. While I was manipulating it through the gate Keith came running out of the house and went into muttered conference with his brother. They were about as unlike as a pea and a bean in the same pod, for Keith was a wizened and knobbly, gnome-like child, very small for his age and wearing steel-rimmed glasses which so far had done nothing much to counteract a violent squint. Barry was the spokesman:

"He says Mum's upstairs. She's sorry she wasn't ready for you, but she'll be down in five minutes and would you mind waiting in the living room?"

"Not at all, if you'll show me the way."

They both escorted me as far as the living room, which was large and antiseptic, with no visible speck of dust anywhere and with a picture window overlooking the garden and the meadow beyond it. The curtains were made of natural hessian and the predominating colour of the furnishings was muted beige.

There wasn't an ashtray in sight, so I didn't dare light a cigarette and the only books were contained in a small and lonely shelf and consisted mainly of technical works about film making. The other titles were equally unalluring as they all referred to wild birds or sailing.

Luckily the reading matter on the coffee table was more my style, for along with a neat pile of women's magazines it included a copy of the *South Berkshire Herald and Gazette* and I spent an enjoyable ten minutes catching up with all the recent weddings and bazaars, plus the rather mysterious case of the man who had been fined two pounds by the magistrates' court for insulting behaviour in the public swimming baths, although the form it had taken was tantalisingly withheld.

Still no sign of Brenda, so I turned to the back page, which was entirely devoted to the For Sale, Hire & Wanted and Miscellaneous columns. These usually provide plenty of fun and there was an added fascination this time because several of the small ads for boats had been marked with a cross. I read each of these with special care, in the vague hope of coming across some clue to Mike's state of mind immediately before his disappearance. The exercise was not entirely unrewarding for it showed at least that he had approached the task in a spirit of great confidence and optimism. There was even a two-berth, sea-going cabin cruiser, with cooker, open to offers, which had a tick against it. Another small diversion was provided by the fact that one advertisement included in this department and beginning: Boats, Trains, Planes . . . actually turned out to refer to something called the Four Corners Travel Bureau, which would presumably mean a rap over the knuckles for some feckless member of the staff.

At this point in the literary feast the door opened and Brenda entered the room.

She appeared more composed than at our last meeting, with the defenceless look less in evidence, but this was no great improvement because the truculence had become correspondingly more pronounced and her greeting was curt:

"Sorry to have kept you, but I understood you to say you wouldn't be here till eleven, and there's a lot for one person to do in a house this size, especially with the boys at home all day."

As a reception it could be said to lack warmth and for two pins I would have driven straight back to London and left her to sort out her own troubles. Only past gratitude to Mike and the lingering belief that he might be lying injured or ill somewhere induced me to stick it out. If he were in some kind of trouble and unable to contact his family, then the least I could do was to try and ease the burden on them. It also occurred to me in passing that in Brenda's situation, I too might be somewhat deficient in affability, and so I said:

"Yes, I apologise for disrupting your morning, but I came early because it had struck me that you might need some cash for the weekend shopping. So I've brought enough to tide you over for the next few days."

"Oh no, thanks. It's very good of you, but I couldn't possibly accept it. We hardly know each other and I'm not asking for charity."

"Now, listen to me, Brenda," I began and then doggedly ploughed through my full repertoire of persuasive argument, countering all her objections and practically going on my knees to get her accept my measly twenty pounds, which at the end of ten minutes solid work she grudgingly consented to do.

"So now I'll leave you in peace," I said when she had tucked the money away in her bag, but it seemed that the completion of this sordid transaction had cleared the air for her because, much to my surprise, she said in a friendlier tone:

"No, please don't go. Not unless you're in a tearing hurry. If you can spare a moment, I'd like your opinion on this letter I've just found."

"Don't tell me! You mean he left a note, after all?"

"No, nothing like that. This isn't from Mike. It was something I came across in one of his suit pockets. You know, Tessa, when I found he'd drawn out all that money and left us with nothing to live on it was like an awful smack in the face. It completely knocked me out; but then I began to think that he must have had it in his mind to go for a long time and, if only I were to try hard enough, I'd remember something or find something which might give me a clue as to where he'd gone. It didn't seem possible that he could keep me in the dark like that, leading what you might call a double life for weeks, or maybe months on end, without making a mistake somewhere. So that was what made me search through all his pockets."

"And you found a letter?"

"Not a whole one. Here, see what you think! It was in the inside pocket of his dark suit, which he only wears about once in a blue moon, so goodness knows how long it's been there."

She opened her bag again and extracted what looked like a torn off half sheet of deep blue writing paper. I took it eagerly, but was disappointed to find that the words on it conveyed nothing whatever. They appeared to be merely half a dozen trade names, with measurements and prices set against each of them.

"Not that side," Brenda said impatiently, "turn it over."

I did so, turning it sideways as well, for just below the wider and torn off edge there was a single line of writing in large italic script, with a signature beneath, which ran as follows:

'. . . *yours for the rest of my life,*

Chloe'

"What do you make of that?" Brenda asked.

"I don't know," I said, reading the words again and finding no more comfort in them. "Part of a letter, obviously. Pity you didn't find the rest of it."

"He must have destroyed it. Probably didn't realise this was on the back when he jotted down those notes. But, listen! You moved much more in his world than I did when you get right down to it, and what I've been plucking up courage to ask you is this: do you know anyone called Chloe?"

"Yes, as a matter of fact, I do."

"Ah! So she works at the film studios, does she?"

"Yes, in the art department. Supposed to be very talented. Of course it doesn't have to be the same one, but Chloe is not such a common name and there's also the fact that Mike must know her too. I never heard they were particularly friendly though."

"What's her other name?"

"I'm trying to remember. It begins with M. Mason or something like that. No, hang on! Masters. Chloe Masters."

"What's she like? Young? Attractive?"

"It's hard to tell, isn't it, but I shouldn't think all that young. She's been around for some time. Twenty-eight or nine, at a guess. I daresay some people find her attractive, but definitely not the sort of girl you'd expect anyone to leave home for, if that's any comfort to you."

Not all of this was strictly accurate, for to those who admired the voluptuous type, Chloe Masters was quite a dish, and I think there must have been a fair number of them too, for while not appearing conceited she was notable for her poise and self-confidence, I remembered her as a bosomy kind of girl, with slender legs which gave her a slightly top heavy look, dark curly hair, sloe eyes and a short upper lip. Nevertheless, my assurances were not wholly insincere, being based principally on the unlikelihood of someone of Chloe's character running away with such a dim little man as Mike Parsons, so it amounted to the same thing. Naturally, I was also aware that the tiny snag in this thinking lay in the faint chance that Chloe, having moved around a bit, was now ready to settle for one who possessed those qualities of undemanding kindness and generosity, which were so conspicuous in Mike, but I did not feel the necessity to pass these reservations on to Brenda.

"Is she married?" Brenda asked and I guessed from the edginess of her tone that she was putting the question for the second time.

"I couldn't be sure, but I believe not. I hardly know her, but I've never heard anyone mention a husband. Also I've got what they call a photographic memory and I don't visualise her wearing a wedding ring. In fact," I went on on a note of triumph as studious concentration brought results, "I have a flickering idea that someone told me she was engaged to be married, but it fizzled out for some reason. There was an invalid mother to support, or a dotty sister, or something of that kind. So on the whole, she doesn't sound at all the sort of person who'd elope with someone else's husband."

"Well, if you ask me, it was a funny sort of letter to be writing to someone else's husband."

"I know, but let us not get carried away, Brenda. We can't be sure that she's the same Chloe and we haven't read the whole of it. It could have been completely innocent."

"You think so, do you? Would you feel like that if you'd found it in your husband's pocket?"

There were so many unanswerables in this question that I skipped them all, saying airily:

"Well, there's one obvious way to tackle it."

"What's that?"

"By making a few enquiries. If it should turn out that Chloe Masters has skipped too, then you've got your answer."

"And how am I to set about that, I should like to know? Not having heard of the woman until you told me about her, I wouldn't even know where to start."

"Alec Ferguson might know," I said, understanding even as I spoke what is meant by putting a rod in pickle.

"Yes, he might, but I can see myself asking him! I've had about as much as I can stand from that one."

Tears of self-pity welled in her eyes and watching her wipe them away I could tell, down to the last syllable, what she would say next:

"I suppose you wouldn't . . . ?"

"Me?"

"Well, it would be different if you asked him. He wouldn't dare be cheeky to you."

I sighed. "It's not really my business, Brenda."

"No man is an island," she answered sharply, taking me aback a little. "That's what Mike used to say. Mind you, I always thought it was a load of rubbish. I thought if any man was an island it was him but I was wrong, wasn't I? He wasn't an island at all. He was one of those what do you call it . . . peninsulars, that's right . . . and the only part I knew was the very tip at the end."

There was a brief silence while we both meditated on this sad judgement and then she returned to the attack.

"You see, I can't help feeling it would be such a help in tracing him if we knew for certain that he'd gone off with this Chloe person. After all, it would be much harder for two people to hide out than one on his own; but I don't want to drag in the police and then it should turn out she'd done nothing wrong, do I? It's not that I want Mike back if he doesn't want to come, don't think that. I hope I'd have more pride. Only it seems so unfair that he should get away with it scot-free, leaving us in the lurch without a penny to our names. What sort of life would it be, bringing up two boys on national assistance? We'd have to leave our home, that's the first thing. I couldn't afford to keep up the payments even if we were legally entitled to go on living here."

"Couldn't you get a job of some kind?"

"Yes, I suppose I could do that. I did go on working part time when I was first married, so I'm not all that rusty, but it would still be an awful struggle, wouldn't it? And it's so unfair. I think Mike ought to be made to see that he's got to contribute something to our support. That's not asking too much, is it?"

"Not too much," I admitted.

"And you see, you being an actress and everything, you could easily worm it out of Mr Ferguson without him seeing what your game was."

Nothing in this programme appealed to me very deeply, for worming things out of Alec Ferguson, still more playing games with him ranked among the principle activities I had hoped to get through life without engaging in. However, I recognised that I had brought it on myself by getting involved in the first place and there was small hope of backing out now. Furthermore, although I did not find Brenda particularly endearing, I did feel a profound pity for her and was constantly reminding myself that it was unfair to judge, without ever having had an opportunity to see her at her best.

One small incident which occurred just as I was leaving did much to harden this view, for it proved beyond any doubt that her veneer of composure was paper thin and that her new hard practicality certainly did not spring from indifference.

It happened as we were walking out to the car and the lawn at the side of the house came into view again. The boys were still there, but they had exchanged their bicycles for another form of transport. Barry was lolling back in a wheelbarrow, while his younger brother laboriously trundled him around, his small form bent double between the handles and his weedy legs splayed out behind him.

The most extraordinary transformation came over Brenda as she took in this rather comical scene. The colour left her face, her eyes stared in horror and she began to tremble as violently as when she first came to see me. Then, as the wheelbarrow completed a wobbly half-turn and made what appeared to be an involuntary plunge in our direction, she let fly:

"Put him down! Put him down this minute, do you hear me, Keith? He's much too heavy for you."

Keith instantly let go of his end of the barrow, which tilted sideways, so that Barry rolled out on to the grass. Scarlet with humiliation he shambled towards us.

"It's all right, Mum, we weren't doing any harm and it was his idea."

"I don't care whose idea it was, you ought to have more sense. Great boy like you, what do you think you're doing, letting him push you around? He could do himself an injury."

"No, he couldn't," Keith muttered truculently, "He was light as a feather."

"And just look at you!" Brenda shouted, changing tactics and beating furiously at some leaves and twigs which had stuck to Barry's jersey. "Getting yourself all filthy like that! As though I hadn't enough to do! You ought to be ashamed of yourself!"

She was certainly making a big production of it and as the barrow was a very light weight, rubber-wheeled contraption, I concluded that it was a case of venting her own misery and frustration on the nearest victim. Fortunately the tirade soon wore itself out, subsiding to a muttered, generalised grumble, before she finally smoothed down Barry's hair in a vaguely affectionate gesture and dismissed him:

"Now, run along, both of you and open the gate for Miss Crichton. And don't ever let me catch you playing such tricks again, there's good boys."

"Sorry to fly off the handle like that," she added, turning to me as they scampered away. "I don't know what's got into me, but the slightest thing seems to set me off these days."

"I can well understand that," I told her. "Obviously, it was seeing the wheelbarrow that upset you."

"Yes, it was," she answered in a muffled tone, covering her face with her hands and leaning against the bonnet in an attitude of utter despair. "How did you guess?"

"Oh well, it's become a horrible sort of symbol for you, I daresay. The sight of it standing by the hedge last Tuesday morning was where it all began."

She did not immediately reply, but remained almost supine over the car, only her shoulders heaving slightly and I guessed she was fighting off a fresh outburst of hysteria. She won through too, for after a short but uncomfortable silence she straightened up, wiping her eyes with the back of her hand and said in a flat voice:

"Silly of me, I know, but seeing the boys larking about with it just then touched off a nerve somewhere and I couldn't stop myself. I ought not to snap at them, poor kids, things are bad enough without that, but it's this strain and uncertainty which are getting me down. If only I knew where he'd gone and what made him do it, I think I could bear it better, but things just keep going round and round in my head and I never get any nearer to finding out where I went wrong and what's to become of us now."

"Try not to worry," I said feebly. "The police are bound to trace him now that they've got the car number, and I'll do all I can on the other front."

"Thanks. Just have to keep hoping for the best, I suppose," she said abruptly and then turned and walked back to the house.

If any further stiffening of the resolve to do my best for them had been needed, it was provided by the sight of puny little Keith swinging on the wrought iron gate, while Barry, stern and pink in the face, guided me out on to the lane with all the cool, self-conscious authority of a policeman clearing a passage for royalty through the Piccadilly traffic.

Brenda might well be partly responsible for the mess she was landed in, but nobody, in my opinion, had the right to play such a mean trick on this pair.

CHAPTER FIVE

FOR all his pawky, pompous manner, Alec Ferguson did not lack shrewdness and I considered that Brenda had rather over-estimated my talents with her airy assumption that he would fail to see through any little game that presented itself on the spur of the moment for the worming process. I therefore planned my strategy well in advance.

Having fixed myself up to lunch at the studios with a coarse-grained, foul-mouthed and utterly dear old cameraman, with whom it was a pleasure as well as sound policy to remain on friendly terms, I pattered along at the end of this agreeable session and presented myself at the studio manager's office, where I knew I should find Alec poring over breakdowns and costing schedules, of whose composition he made such heavy weather. I tapped on the door and, responding with all speed to his peremptory "Come!" entered the room just fast enough to see him slide the current crossword puzzle into the top drawer of his desk. He then gave me a long, severe and enquiring look and requested me to take a seat while he finished off a wee ticklish job he was up to his neck in.

He continued the ready reckoning for a few minutes, no doubt asking himself the purpose of my visit, and no doubt also sending back the answers as quick as a flash, so I trust that when he finally leant back in his chair and invited me to proceed, I managed to take some of the wind out of his sails.

"I have come to ask you a favour," I explained.

"You have, have you? And what would that be?"

"Well, not so much you as your secretary."

"Sally? Where does she come into it?"

"Everywhere, but naturally I could hardly ask her to do a little job for me without getting your permission first."

"What job? I don't think I follow you."

"No, of course you don't, but it's like this, Alec: the week after next will be our wedding anniversary, the 29th to be precise, and Robin and I are giving a party."

"Congratulations!"

"Thank you, and I hope you'll be able to come. Your wife too, I need hardly say."

"I'll have to check on that. I don't know of anything to prevent us, but I must clear it with Madge, you understand?"

"Oh yes, no hurry at all. I'll be sending you a card in a day or two, but the reason I've come to see you is this: we thought it would be a nice idea to drum up as many as we can of the people we've both been working with during the past year. It's going to be rather a funny gathering; with all Robin's coppers from the Yard mixed up with my lot, but we thought it might be fun."

"A curious idea of fun, in my opinion."

"Oh, why?"

"Some people might not be too pleased to find themselves rubbing shoulders with the law. My own conscience is clear enough, but I couldn't vouch for all my colleagues."

"But this is to be a party, Alec. They won't be flashing their notebooks at everyone and asking them where they've hidden the body and how they fudged last year's income tax returns. In fact, if you imagine policemen don't behave exactly like everyone else when they're off duty, it's really high time you met some. Besides, Robin and I are rather bored by this thing of keeping our friends in separate compartments just because they happen to work in different spheres."

"Well, I can't tell you whether we'll be able to come or not. I rather feel we've got something on that week. In fact, I'm pretty certain Madge did mention something about it only the other day. But what had you in mind for Sally? Not sending out the invitations, I hope? If so, I'll have to say no to that right away. We've both got a lot on our plates just now."

"Oh, goodness, Alec, I wouldn't dream of asking such a thing. Surely you know me better than that? It's just that I've got three or four people on my list who present a problem. None of them appears to be working here today, otherwise I wouldn't need to bother you."

"What kind of problem?"

"Addresses, mainly. They're either ex-directory or they live out of London, because I can't find them in the book. I thought Sally would be bound to have them on her files and it wouldn't take her a minute to look them up. Also I've put a tick against two of them who may be married and I thought she could probably put me right on that as well."

"Let's have a look at this list of yours," Alec said, stretching out his hand.

I had been to some trouble in compiling it and was able to pass it over with barely a tremor. He perused it in silence, pursing his lips and running a finger down the side of his nose, until eventually he said:

"Well, you can save yourself the trouble, so far as two of these are concerned. You'd very likely be wasting your time."

"Which two?"

"Parsons, for a start."

"Oh damn! I particularly wanted to throw a little hospitality in Mike's way."

"You'd be ill-advised to throw too much of it in Mrs Mike's, however. Even your off duty policemen might feel a little uncomfortable with an alcoholic at the feast."

"Oh, but I thought she'd got over that now? Someone told me she was much better."

"Did they now? Well, that's not what I've heard, and I fancy Mike would be rather surprised to hear it too. In any case, it's my impression they've split up."

"Is that so? Well, perhaps Mike would come on his own."

"Perhaps."

"You're very mysterious, Alec. Don't you know where he is?"

"No, I must confess I don't. He was here last Monday, finishing off a rush job and that's the last we've seen of him. He asked for the day off on Tuesday but he didn't show up on Wednesday either and he hasn't been back since. It's these little vagaries on the part of the staff which make it so tough for blokes like me who have to keep the wheels turning."

"And no word of explanation?"

"Not one. And his wife's been on the telephone to me in a fine old state. She's no more idea than I have where he is, which gives me the idea that the worm has finally turned."

"Oh, do you really think so, Alec? I mean, couldn't he just have gone off somewhere quietly on his own for a few days to relax? After all, he's been doing a lot of overtime lately . . ."

I broke off because Alec was looking at me with an expression I could not fully interpret, although there was a new alertness in it and a trace of fear as well.

"Who told you he'd been doing a lot of overtime lately?" he asked quietly.

"Can't remember . . . yes, I can, it was someone I was talking to in the restaurant just now. Why? Isn't it true?"

"Not so far as I know and I fancy I might have heard about it. Mind you, I'm not saying it isn't the kind of tale his wife might have come out with, but then you couldn't have heard it from her, could you?"

"No, of course not. Oh well, I'll just have to put a question mark against his name and hope he turns up in time for the party. Which was the other name you said I should scrub?"

"What? Oh yes, let's see now . . . yes, here we are, Chloe Masters."

"Well, don't tell me Chloe's left home too?" I asked, hoping the merry laughter didn't sound overdone.

"Not as far as I know."

"Then why mustn't I invite her?"

"Och, I didn't say that. I don't believe she'll be available, that's all."

"Why, Alec? What's the matter with her?"

"Nothing's the matter with her. In fact she was working here until a week or two ago. Then she asked me to find a temporary replacement for her. It seems her brother was due to come out of hospital and she has to stay at home for a while and look after him."

"Oh, it's her brother, is it? What's wrong with him?"

"Some muscular complaint, I understand. He's had it since birth."

"Incurable?"

"So I believe. He used to be in a home for the physically handicapped, but he went into a hospital for an operation some while back. Chloe told me it hadn't been all that successful and she's got him on her hands for the time being."

"Why's that? Has she no parents?"

"I really couldn't tell you. I'm not a wet nurse, you know, however much it may look like it sometimes. And, if you'll excuse me now, I have work to do. I'll ask Sally to look up the other people on your list and she'll probably give you a ring at home. Suit you?"

"Okay," I said, accepting my dismissal. "And thanks for your help, but please ask her to let me have Chloe's address too. I can at least try and it may be specially important for her not to feel cut off from everyone just now."

"Oh, you can try," Alec said indifferently. "But for my money it won't get you anywhere."

Privately I agreed with him but as it happened we were both wrong, for when Sally telephoned me later that day to give me Chloe's address, along with several others which I dutifully wrote down, it marked the first major step forward in solving the mystery of Mike's disappearance.

CHAPTER SIX

BEFORE this happened there had been developments from another quarter, which so far from clarifying matters had cast them into even deeper obscurity, seeming to sever the last remaining link with our quarry.

It was Robin who brought the news. He had arrived home later than usual on Monday evening in a rather disgruntled frame of mind and was not noticeably cheered up to learn that the following Sunday week was our wedding anniversary and that I had more or less committed us to celebrating it with a rather ill-assorted party.

"I thought our wedding anniversary was in October?" he asked in mild surprise.

"Usually it is, but not this year."

"Oh Lord!"

"Never mind. You don't have to give me a present. I can wait until October for that."

"I would rather give you the Hope diamond than play host at the kind of party you have just described." Recalling with faint misgivings that it was exactly one week to the day that Mike Parson's had also arrived home tired and dispirited after the long day's grind and had shortly afterwards walked out of it again, never to return, I made haste to put aside the depressing prospect of the party and to seek out sunnier topics.

Apparently I did not entirely succeed, for having allowed me to prattle on for about five minutes, he finally came out of a reverie and interrupted me in mid-sentence: "By the way, Tess, I have some news for you too."

"Good news?"

"You may think so. They've found your friend's car."

"Mike's? Honestly? Where was it?"

"In a road called the Strand. Not the London one, this is a cul de sac on the outskirts of Reading, a few miles below the bridge."

"When was it found?"

"If you mean when was it traced to the owner, the answer is this morning. I'd asked the local branch to keep me informed as a personal favour and they did."

"But they don't know how long the car had been there?"

"Right. Although it was certainly not less than three days. It was parked a few yards from where the road comes to a full stop at the river. There aren't many houses around because for most of its length on one side the Strand borders the cemetery of a Roman Catholic church, but there's a little pub called the Angler's Rest on the opposite side. Naturally, there's no through traffic, but there are nearly always a few cars parked there at various times of the day and night, quite often a dozen or more at this time of year with so many holiday-makers around. You see, there's a small landing stage and a man who hires out boats in a modest way, so anyone taking one of those out would naturally park as close as he could get to the river. Not much chance of anyone noticing that one particular car had been left there for several days running."

"Nevertheless, someone did notice, I gather. Was it this boatman?"

"No, he only has his business there, doesn't live on the premises and didn't know a thing about it. At least the only item he did come up with doesn't appear to have any relevance."

"What was it?"

"One of his punt poles is missing, apparently. Past experience has made him careful to take all the paddles and cushions in at night, but this was the first time that anyone had helped himself to a punt pole. It's hard to say how there could be any connection between that and the abandoned car."

"Well, who did notice the car?"

"A man called Jackson, who is the publican at the Angler's Rest. The brewer's dray called on Thursday morning with deliveries and the driver had a bit of trouble turning round when it was time to leave because this particular vehicle made it doubly awkward for him. No one was particularly bothered by that because it happens all the time, but it did focus Jackson's attention on the car and when he found it was still parked there right through the weekend he reported it."

"Any clues inside the car?"

"I haven't had full details yet, but there were a couple of odd features for all to see."

"Do tell me."

"A man's tweed jacket on the front seat and the keys in the ignition. It was a miracle the car wasn't stolen."

"Perhaps it was intended to be. I mean, if you think of it, Robin, the jacket could have been left there as a bait. So that anyone of dubious morality who happened to pass by and take a look inside would immediately see it and then moving in to take a closer look would see the keys too, and away we go!"

"But what reason could he have had for wanting it to be stolen?"

"Well, I've always thought his first move would be to dispose of the car, and he probably thought this way would be less risky than trying to sell it."

"Rather an expensive way out of the problem, don't you think? They tell me the second-hand value is around five or six hundred pounds and even if he was willing to drop that amount in order to cover his tracks, why throw in the jacket as well. Why not just cut his losses and abandon the car somewhere where it wouldn't be so easily found?"

"I think I have an answer for that," I said.

"Somehow, I thought you might."

"He may have wanted the car to be stolen, so that there was a chance of its eventually getting back to his wife more or less in one piece. If it had been locked up and left in some lonely place all sorts of disasters might have befallen it before the police came around. I mean, like the battery and wheels being pinched and that kind of thing. By making it so easy and accessible he may have been trying to ensure that it would still be in reasonable condition when it was restored to his wife. Assuming he was feeling guilty about leaving her virtually penniless, it would have been some consolation to know that she would have the car or, to put it another way, the means of raising five or six hundred pounds. Tell me something, though: were the log book and insurance certificate in the car, by any chance?"

"Yes, they were. In a pocket of the jacket."

"Well, doesn't that prove my point?"

"No."

"Oh, really?" I asked sadly. "What have I overlooked?"

"Well, to be fair, I think your theory is all right up to a point, but it doesn't go nearly far enough."

"Then take it a little further for me, please."

"Well, if you think back to what I told you about the Strand, you'll realise that abandoning the car in that particular spot gives strong indications that his intention was suicide. The landing stage juts out into fairly deep water, naturally, so where better to dive in if you'd made up your mind to finish yourself off that way?"

"But, of course! You must be right and in some ways suicide does seem so much more . . ."

"In character?"

"Exactly. More in character than leaving home for another woman. How nice to find that psychology has its place, after all. Is that what the police believe did happen?"

"No, they don't."

"Well, for God's sake, Robin!"

"They have to operate without your special kind of insight, remember, but from the meagre evidence at their disposal, they incline to the view that he intended everyone to believe that he had committed suicide, but had not in fact done so."

"Well, that's sophistry, if you like! Why the hell make it so complicated?"

"Because of the very point you overlooked earlier. If he really went to all that trouble to ensure that his wife got the car back in good condition, why not just have left it in the garage and killed himself in some other way? And why draw out the full balance in their joint account? If his aim was suicide he could achieve it just as efficiently without three hundred pounds in his pocket."

"It might have been pinched from the pocket of his jacket which they found in the car?"

"Yes, darling, so it might," Robin explained with deep and unflagging patience, "and most likely the jacket was left there to give precisely that impression, but I repeat: if he was suicide bent, why draw it out at all?"

"Yes, I see all that, I'm not a complete imbecile," I replied crossly. "But he could have changed his mind, you know. Supposing, having decided to leave Brenda, he'd then become absolutely sickened by the idea? Once he'd actually made the break it might have come over him that although there was no future for him with her there was no future for him on his own either. Perhaps the suicide idea was just a sudden impulse? Who knows what desperate ideas might take hold of someone in that situation?"

"Who indeed? And if you're right and he is dead we shall never have the faintest inkling about his state of mind during the last hours, so it is really useless to speculate."

"All right then, to consider it on the practical level: if he did drown, how long will it be before he is found?"

"And that's the hardest of all to answer," Robin admitted. "Presumably, it could be never and it could on the other hand be tomorrow, when some small boy fishing from the bank gets his line entangled with a human foot. So much would depend on weeds and currents and that kind of thing."

"But since the police tend to discount suicide, what will they do next about tracing him?"

"Ah, an easy one at last! The answer is nothing."

"What, nothing at all?"

"No, nothing at all. Why should they? As I've tried to make you understand, he's committed no crime. The money he took was his own property and in this country, thank God, a man is still entitled to privacy. I suppose they might get him for leaving his car unattended on a public thoroughfare but it would hardly be worth the trouble and if he wishes to hide himself away there is nothing whatever to stop him."

Given time, I might conceivably have found a flaw in this argument, but the opportunity was denied me because it was at this point that Sally rang up to give me Chloe Masters' address.

CHAPTER SEVEN

SHE lived at Old Lock Cottage, Warmenham, which, being situated between Cookham and Marlow, was one very good reason for not finding her in the London directory. Presumably the cottage had originally been one of the lock keeper's perks, and the prefix had been tacked on to its name when this function became outdated. The present incumbent was housed nearby in a square red brick villa, with neat rows of runner beans in the garden adjacent to it, a glorious show of salvias surrounding the patch of lawn which separated it from Warmenham Lock, and the numerals 1931 carved into the brick work above the door for the benefit of anyone who hadn't already guessed.

Chloe's cottage, which predated the other by a couple of centuries, was fifty yards further down river and set back by the same distance from the bank, although no attempt had been made to profit by the extra space, for the garden was a sad tangle of weeds and starved look- ing shrubs.

With her usual efficiency Sally had supplied me with the telephone number, which was Warmenham 441, but I had not made use of the information. For one thing, I knew the area well and had no need to apply for directions. Warmenham, which consists of a hamlet, several large farms and a few plushy mansions dotted around on the perimeter, is not very far from Storhampton, where Robin and I had spent the first year of our marriage, and only ten or twelve miles from Roakes Common and the home of my cousin Toby.

Another and distinctly more cogent reason for giving no advance warning of my visit was the suspicion that, in the unlikely event of Chloe's being at home to answer the telephone, she would certainly find some excuse to fob me off. Were I to succeed in breaking through this barrier too, the chances of finding any remaining traces of a missing sound recordist would have been rendered very slim indeed.

At first sight it appeared that these precautions had been as superfluous as I had secretly feared, for there were numerous indications that the cottage was at present uninhabited. There was a low, unpainted wooden gate, opening on to a gravel path to the front door and beside it a brick and flint barn, which had been subdivided so as to make one half into a garage, but the doors were wide open and the interior empty.

By contrast, I saw as I walked up the path that not only the front door but all the windows on that side of the cottage were shut. There was no bell or knocker so I banged on the door as hard as I could, but no one came and there was no sound from within. After a minute or two I gently lifted the latch and gave the door a push, but it must have been locked or bolted from inside for it would not budge.

Balked at the outset, I stepped to one side and peered in at one of the ground floor windows, but the pane was

smudged and I could not make out much of the interior. At first sight it appeared to be a dining room, for I
could see a bowl of oranges on a sideboard against the
wall facing me, but when I had got my face practically
flattened against the glass and had brought my hands up
to form side shields, I could see that beside the right-an-
gled wall to my left there was a camp bed, unmade but
recently used apparently for the bedclothes were untidily
pulled back.

Following the path round the side of the cottage I
emerged into the tangled, overgrown back garden. From
this point I could see glimpses of the river and the lock
keeper's new house, although both were partially screened
by half a dozen ancient and barren-looking apple trees.
Two of these had been used as props for a clothes line
and they cannot have been so fragile as they looked, for
it was festooned down the whole of its length with washing, including sheets and towels and an assortment of
men's clothing.

The sight had an instant and chastening effect. All at
once the role I was playing manifested itself as somewhat
despicable, and Robin's words about the individual's
right to privacy came home to me with a shattering jolt.
If Mike wished to leave his rather shrewish little wife and
set up house with Chloe, it was surely his own business
and how on earth, I wondered, forgetting now about the
two sad little boys, had I allowed myself to be coerced
into creeping about and spying on him? Mortified and
ashamed, my instinct was to remove myself from the
scene as fast as possible, but simultaneously there came
another sensation, a prickling at the back of my neck,
which partially paralysed movement. Remaining on the

same spot, I turned very slowly to face the cottage again, thus breaking the record for unpleasant frissons by getting my second in the space of a minute. Through the closed panes of a ground floor window beside the back door a white cadaverous face was staring out at me, evidently transfixed by pain and terror. Seen through glass, it took on a swimmy, disembodied quality, so that I had the impression of looking at a ghost or a corpse, and this was intensified by the fact that as I watched it misted over and slowly receded from sight, as though a wave had passed over and covered it.

At that moment there was nothing that Lady Macbeth could have told me about her disagreeable sensations when Banquo's ghost turned up at the dinner party and I raced back to the front of the house and down the garden path with only one object in view, which was to fling myself into the car and drive away at eighty miles an hour.

The decision had come too late, however, although it was not the supernatural which intervened this time, but the presence of a little orange mini car drawn up behind mine. Just as I reached the gate the driver emerged, looking very cool and composed in her pink linen dress, and I found myself face to face with Chloe Masters.

CHAPTER EIGHT

SHE was carrying a whacking great pile of cardboard folders, with her white bag precariously balanced on top, and I automatically unlatched the gate and then stepped back to allow her to pass through. She thanked me, with a wide and friendly smile, and then said:

"Were you just leaving? What a bit of luck I caught you!"

Somewhat fazed by the choice of words, I brought an envelope out of my bag and said, with no enthusiasm at all:

"I only called to deliver this. It's an invitation to our party and I happened to be passing, so I thought I might as well drop it in. Save postage and all that."

Realising, if only from her amused expression, that this explanation left something to be desired, I went on:

"I couldn't make anyone hear when I knocked and I was just going to push my card under the door when it occurred to me that you might be in the garden, so I went to look, but of course you weren't there either and . . ."

"Won't you come inside and tell me the rest sitting down?"

"Oh no, thanks awfully, Chloe, I'm sure you've got masses to do."

"No, I haven't. All I've got to do is read your card and tell you whether I can come to the party or not, thereby saving myself some postage too. Besides, these scripts weigh a ton. My arms will drop off if I don't put them down soon."

"Shall I carry some of them for you?" I asked, bowing to her superior control of the situation.

"No, I can manage. If you'd just be an angel and unlock the door? The key's in my bag."

"I suppose you always have to lock up when you go out and leave the house empty?" I asked in what was supposed to be an innocent voice, as she preceded me into the tiny hall. It was a waste of innocence, however, for she either did not hear or chose to ignore the question and walked ahead of me into a room on the right, twin brother to the one I had peered at from outside. It was a low ceilinged, untidy but comfortable looking sitting room, with an inglenook fireplace and a welter of blackened oak beams.

"What would you like?' she asked, dumping her load on to a gate legged table in the window, which already held a typewriter, telephone and pile of books. "We've no booze in the house, I'm afraid, but I can offer you some coffee or a soft drink?"

I had noticed that she did not seem particularly surprised to see me and, being in the mood to come straight to the point, I said, when she returned from the kitchen with the coffee tray:

"You don't seem particularly surprised to see me?"

"No, Alec warned me that you were on my trail."

"Warned you?"

"Well, that doesn't sound very polite, I admit; but there was something rather sly in the way he put it, if you know what I mean? Not exactly winks and nods and verb saps, but as though he meant me to infer something and be on my guard. I can't imagine why."

"But I thought you'd stopped going to the studios for the time being?"

"So I have, but the script department is being very decent and they let me have stacks of stuff to read at home. It's a frightful chore, as you can imagine, and it doesn't pay very well, but it's better than nothing and I hate to be idle. It was when I went over to fetch this new batch that I ran into Alec."

She had been opening my envelope while explaining this and now continued without a change of tone,

"Well, that's very civil of you! Do you want an answer now?"

"No, no hurry at all. It's quite informal."

"The trouble is that Sunday evenings are apt to be tricky because I don't know whether my neighbour will be able to oblige for an hour or two. It's a busy period on the lock gates when the weather's fine and she sometimes has to be on hand to help. You see, I've got my invalid brother here at present."

"Yes, I did hear. How's he getting on?"

"Not at all well. He can't be left on his own for very long, especially after dark. His nerves are completely shattered, unfortunately. It's not that he needs company, but he's virtually helpless and terrified of being alone in the house, in case the bogeyman calls. As you've just seen, I have to lock him in whenever I do have to go out. It's the only way he feels at all safe."

"It must be frightful for you. I am sorry."

"Oh, I expect I'll survive," Chloe said, getting up and tossing the invitation card on to the typewriter before re-filling her cup. "Can I top you up too?"

I joined her by the table, thinking hard and fingering the card as she poured me out some more coffee. There was something derisory, almost contemptuous in her manner which had gone far towards overcoming my earlier scruples and to send me veering over to Brenda's side again, and it prompted me to say:

"You'd better write down my telephone number on the back of this, Chloe. Then you'll be able to call me up some time and let me know whether you can come or not."

She turned the card over and wrote the number as I dictated it. It was reasonably conclusive, but to make absolutely sure I added hastily:

"And now put 'after seven, or lunch time, and ask for Robin, if I should be out'," throwing in all the wordy detail I could think of, in order to get a fair specimen of her handwriting. When it was done I went on:

"I've just remembered one other thing I meant to ask you: have you had any news of Mike Parsons?"

Chloe dropped her pen on the table and replied in a matching throwaway voice:

"I heard rumours that he'd left his wife, which, if true, doesn't surprise me in the least."

"Oh, really? I wouldn't have said she was that bad."

"Don't misunderstand me. I've never laid eyes on her and I know nothing about her, except that she's reputed to be an alcoholic, which doesn't surprise me either. What I meant was that it was just the kind of lousy trick that Mike would play."

And considering that this was just about the most unlikely remark I had expected to hear, I felt that I managed to conceal my astonishment reasonably well.

"Why do you say that? I've always found him such a kind little man."

"Oh, he's kind all right. That's the trouble."

"I don't understand you," I said, walking away from the table and sitting down again. "You say you're not surprised and yet how could it be called kind to abandon a wife and two young children, especially when he's always kept them tucked them in such an isolated compartment that now he's gone they have no one to turn to?"

Chloe, who had also returned to her chair, regarded me coolly over the top of her cup.

"It beats me why you seem to have a stake in this, but before you get any further involved it might be as well to set the record straight about Mike."

"I agree, although I haven't become involved of my own volition. It was simply that his wife came to me in great distress and asked me to help her. I had met her once before at a studio party and that was why she picked on me. She thought I might know who Mike's friends were and perhaps find some clue through them as to what had become of him. I felt sorry for her and he's always been the soul of kindness to me, so the least I could do was to make some effort in that direction. Which reminds me, Chloe: did you ever hear him mention someone called Sandy?"

"Never, as far as I recall. Why? Is he another like me who has been marked down to assist the dreary little woman in tracing her runaway husband?"

"Not necessarily," I replied. "And I hadn't specially placed you in that category either," which was true, in so far as I had kept an open mind on the subject until I saw her handwriting.

"Alec didn't throw out any hints?"

"No, certainly not."

"I see. So in that case you struck lucky because there does happen to be a great deal I can tell you about Mike, if you're interested. On the other hand, you may not be because none of it will throw the faintest light on his present whereabouts."

"I would be interested to hear why you appear to dislike him so much."

"And so you shall. To begin with, what you patently have not grasped is that this kindness of his is carried well beyond the bounds of sanity. It has become a mania with him and he not only has to be kind, often in a ridiculous unnecessary way, he also has to be seen to be kind. None of your doing good by stealth for Mr Parsons."

Naturally I regarded this as an exaggeration, possibly emanating from spite, and yet I had to concede that in my own experience of this characteristic of Mike's he had not, finally, left me in ignorance of the enormity of his self-sacrifice or the extent of my indebtedness to him. So I did not argue and Chloe went on:

"God knows what's made him like this. Some deep rooted sense of failure or inferiority complex, for all I know, but the fact is that whatever natural, spontaneous kindness he may have started out with has now become a consuming passion. It's more of a weapon than a virtue."

"A weapon for what?"

"Power, probably. I know what I'm talking about, believe me, Tessa, and I think it works like this; he begins by going out of his way to do someone a great big favour, usually at some cost or inconvenience to himself, and he asks nothing in return except eternal gratitude and admiration. And that, as it often turns out, is quite a lot to ask."

"Most people would be quite content to give it though."

"Oh, I grant you, but it doesn't stop there, you see. With all this loving trust and helping hand around, the next time they find themselves in a spot of trouble they naturally turn to him. And he's oh, so delighted to move heaven and earth to get them on their feet again. So very delighted, in fact, that imperceptibly they feel almost a compulsion to ask him for help, as the one means they know of giving him pleasure. It's as though they tried to express their gratitude by burdening themselves with an even bigger load of it, and of course he uses it to insinuate himself still further into their lives. In no time at all they find they've practically been taken over."

"Well, that's not been my experience at all,' I said, feeling on firmer ground here. 'It's true that he once did go out of his way to do me a very good turn, and perhaps it did rather exceed what was necessary. I mean that he didn't really have to drive an extra sixty or seventy miles just to take me home because I could easily have hired a taxi. In fact, I'd have positively insisted on it if he'd told me before that he had to go all the way back to Reading. So to that extent I'll go along with you, but I can honestly say that since then I've had no special reason to be grateful to him. He's always sympathetic and helpful, but not in an overdone way."

Chloe considered me appraisingly. "Well, perhaps you'd be flying a bit high for him and besides, except for that one occasion, which he described to me with becoming modesty, by the way, you'd make rather a tough proposition. You're doing pretty well in your career and you seem to have got your private life running smoothly too. Presumably, you're not short of money and you don't go in for affairs on the side, so it's hard to see what sort of a jam you could have got yourself into which would send you running to Mr M. Parsons."

"I'd have said you were doing pretty well yourself, come to that."

"You could say so, but unfortunately it doesn't apply to my brother."

"Oh yes, your brother. Is he at the root of all this bitterness?"

Chloe placed her empty cup on a small table, then leant back in her chair and stretched out her elegant, slender legs.

"You know that expression 'killing with kindness'?" she asked me. "In this case, it's literally what happened. You think I'm dramatising it, but Mike has effectively destroyed poor little Johnnie. There's nothing left to him now which is any use to himself or anyone else, which is precisely why I am so delighted to hear that dear Mr Parsons has vanished from the scene. Personally, I hope he's gone a long, long way and will never come back, because so long as he's not around there may still be a chance to pull something out of the wreck."

"Was it your brother I caught a glimpse of through the window just now?"

"Yes. Gave you quite a scare, I expect? Don't worry though, he won't show himself so long as you're here. He can't bear anyone to see him as he is now and he's become terrified of strangers. It's a shame because he used to be such a sweet, trusting sort of boy; amazingly cheerful and friendly, all things considered."

She was forced to break off at this point because the telephone rang. I guessed that, once launched on her story, she resented having to interrupt it, for her responses were laconic to the point of rudeness. As near as I can remember, they went as follows:

"Hallo! . . . Yes . . . I see . . . Yes, very well . . . Yes, goodbye."

She then slammed the receiver down and I said:

"And am I to understand that you blame Mike for the change in him?"

"Most certainly I do and I'll tell you why. You see, poor Johnnie was born with an incurable disease of the spine and he grew up to be a cripple. It affected his brain too. I don't mean that he was an idiot or anything, just slightly retarded and he had to go to a special school, so he didn't get much of an education. On the other hand, they did teach him various simple crafts to keep himself occupied and on the whole he was quite happy. Also my mother adored him. She insisted on keeping him at home, which I think may have been the main reason for my father eventually getting a divorce. It was an awful tie, you see, and they could never go away together unless Johnnie went too. After she died I simply couldn't keep it up. For one thing, I had to earn my living and I soon saw that I hadn't a hope of making any sort of life for myself so long as I was stuck with Johnnie."

"So you put him in a home, I gather?"

"Right. Our own doctor arranged it for me. It was quite a nice place, but of course I felt pretty lousy about it and Johnnie made the most devastating scene when it came to the point. Screaming hysterics for hours on end. I'd never seen him like that and I hadn't even realised that side of him existed."

"But you still went ahead with it?"

"I promised myself that if he was still unhappy after a month I'd bring him home, no matter what, but the miraculous thing was that in less than a week he'd settled in beautifully. He never gave anyone the slightest trouble and he seemed perfectly content. He made lots of friends among the other patients too, and in many ways I think he was much better off than when he was living at home with my mother. I sometimes thought it was too good to last, and I was bloody well right, thanks to Mike and his rotten kindness."

"You surely don't mean that he talked you into having your brother to live with you again?"

"Oh dear me, no, nothing so simple. He's a very devious character, you know, and it all began when he got the full story out of me over a cup of tea one afternoon. That wasn't too difficult because there weren't a great many people I could talk to about it and certainly none who would listen with such sympathy as he did. Among other things, I told him that I made a rule of visiting Johnnie at least once a month, taking him for drives round the countryside and so on; not because I wanted to or that he was ever particularly thrilled to see me, but really to square my own conscience, if you can understand?"

"Oh yes, I can. It's exactly what I'd have done myself."

"Well, anyway, that was where I made my first mistake, because Mike immediately offered to drive me up there the following Saturday. It was around sixty miles there and back and he said it couldn't be much fun for me going on my own, particularly as I was only doing it out of this ghastly puritan sense of duty, and just to have some company on the journey might help. Naturally I was grateful and it did make the whole difference. It was far less of a strain with a third person along and Johnnie took to him at once. The whole thing went off so much more pleasantly that I ignored the red light even when Mike suggested that he should come with me every time I visited. Looking back on it, I could see what an ostrich I'd been. For a man with a family of his own, who hadn't the faintest interest in me personally, that was really too altruistic to make sense. There had to be a catch in it."

"He kept it a close secret from his wife," I remarked. "That is, I mean, I don't think she had the faintest suspicion."

"No, I'm sure of it. I realised when I got to know him better that that has always been his policy. As far as humanly possible, he keeps his life running in separate compartments and if he wants to pursue some course of his own he simply tells her that he's working overtime. For all I know she swallows it, although it might have occurred to her that anyone who chalks up overtime at his rate ought to be a millionaire by now."

"By the way, Chloe, on these outings of yours, I suppose you occasionally went into pubs and so on? Did Mike ever have a drink?"

"No, never. He's completely teetotal, didn't you know?"

"Yes, but from what you've been telling me, he sounds such a different person from the one I know and I just wondered if he'd lied about that too."

"Oh no, that was all on the level. I've an idea he'd been in some kind of accident at one time and it had scared him off alcohol for good, but I forget the details."

"And to get back to you, how long did this situation with your brother go on?"

"About eighteen months. I'd become more than slightly bored with it by then, but having fallen into the routine it was difficult to break it up. Mike was very insistent about keeping things as they were and although I could have coped with that on its own, there were other complications. You see, Johnnie had developed such a crush on him by this time that he passionately looked forward to our visits. He really used to light up when we arrived. He had so few pleasures that I simply couldn't bring myself to deprive him of this one merely because it had become a nuisance for me. You know, Tessa, I sometimes wonder if most of the harm people do to each other isn't caused by misguided unselfishness."

"And what harm did yours do?" I asked, putting aside the general premise for future consideration. "So far, it all sounds reasonably satisfactory."

"Oh, sure, but unfortunately that wasn't enough for Mike. Perhaps he had begun to feel we were taking him too much for granted and the halo was growing a bit dim, for the upshot was that one Saturday morning on the drive up he told me about some article he'd read in the *Lancet*. It was by a surgeon who'd been experimenting with a new kind of operation for spinal complaints and Mike wanted, or pretended to want, my permission to find out more about it."

"Why do you say 'pretended'?"

"Because I suspect that he had already gone quite deeply into it before he even broached it. I told him to go ahead if he wanted to, but that people were always coming up with these so-called miracle cures they'd heard about, whereas our own doctor, who is no doddering old stick-in-the-mud, was convinced that none of them could do Johnnie any good. However, I was beginning to get Mike's form by this time and I did make one firm stipulation."

"What was that?"

"That he should not mention a word of it to Johnnie, at least until we had a few more facts to go on."

"I should hardly have thought that needed saying."

"You wouldn't, would you? But you must remember that Mike is so exceptionally kind. He can't wait to bring hope and cheer into people's lives."

"You can't mean . . . ?"

"Oh yes, I can. He went up to visit Johnnie one week day without bothering to tell me. The patients aren't allowed out of the grounds except with relatives, so Mike spent the afternoon pushing him around the garden in his wheel chair and filling him up with all this rubbish about how he'd have to spend a few weeks in hospital and then he'd be able to swim and play football just like any other boy, and probably later on he'd get married and have some children of his own. Oh, I can't tell you the absurdities! And the heartbreaking thing was that Johnnie swallowed it whole. Mike was his hero and whatever he said was gospel."

"So what did you do?"

"What could I do? He was right up in the clouds with happiness and how could I be the one to drag him down? He would always have believed that I had taken away his one chance of being cured."

"But surely the specialist, if not your own doctor, could have made him understand that this was just a pipe dream?"

"Well, that was my lifeline, actually. I agreed that he should see this surgeon and I said that I'd abide by his decision. If he honestly considered that Johnnie had a chance I wouldn't do anything to oppose it. I guessed the poor boy was in for a crushing disappointment, but at least it would come from an outsider and not from me. But of course nothing is ever simple, is it? Doctors will never make the ultimate decision, you can't really expect them to. All they will do is present you with the facts and leave you to make up your own mind. In this case, we were told that there was a fifty-fifty chance of the operation making a partial improvement in muscular coordination, but we were also warned that there was a one per cent chance of things going horribly wrong. I must say that really scared me, but Mike was quite undaunted. He said that surgeons always threw in that sort of warning, even when it was just a straightforward case of taking someone's tonsils out. They had to do it to cover themselves against the million to one chance of a patient's heart giving out, or something of that kind. Well, you can guess what happened?"

"The million to one chance came off?"

"Right. Not that his heart let him down. In fact, I'm given to understand that all the vital organs are in fine shape and he'll probably live to a ripe old age which is a big comfort, isn't it? But in all other ways he's much worse off now than before and the most terrifying thing of all is the personality change. Nothing left now of the rather sweet-natured creature he used to be; just a snivelling, quivering jelly."

"And no hope at all?"

"Very little. They kept him in the orthopaedic hospital for about six weeks, after which they told me there was nothing more they could do for him and I could take him home at ten o'clock the following morning. Thanks a lot!"

"And what about Mike?"

"What about him? Haven't you heard enough?"

"I just wondered what his reactions were, whether he'd tried to make amends in any way?"

"Oh, he made regular visits to the hospital at first, but they soon dropped off when it became clear what a mess his damned meddling had landed us in. There hasn't been a word from him for the last couple of weeks and that's all the amends I want. The only ray of hope is that as time goes by Johnnie may get back to some of his old form, so that if there should be a vacancy in the home he was in before he'll at least be fit enough to take it up. As long as Mike keeps away there may still be a faint chance for us."

"Yes, I can understand how you must feel. I only wish there was something positive I could do to help."

"Oh, we'll get by, I expect," Chloe said briskly. "No thanks to Mike, but at least the financial situation isn't too grim. I can earn a bit by reading manuscripts and my mother left us this cottage and a half share in a little agency. It's doing pretty well, as it happens, and they've just opened a new branch, so we shan't starve."

"That's one comfort," I said.

"And if you won't mind my saying so, Tessa, the best way you can help is to leave things alone. I should imagine that his wife is far better off without him, and if she doesn't realise that now she soon will. That's mainly why I told you a slight fib just now when you were asking me about someone called Sandy. The fact is, I have heard Mike mention him once or twice and I suppose it was stupid of me to deny it. It was really just a feeble attempt to discourage you from going around questioning any more people. I honestly think that if everyone would mind his own business there'd be a lot less misery in the world."

It was a chastening thought and one which gave me food for reflection as I drove towards the main road. So much so that I found concentration continually slipping away and was thankful when I was at last able to slide out of the London bound traffic by taking a right turn which I knew would eventually lead me through quiet lanes to Toby's house at Roakes Common, where I had invited myself to lunch.

CHAPTER NINE

ONE of Robin's forecasts turned out to be correct in almost every particular, the notable exception being that it was not a small boy who saw the human foot in the water but a twelve-year-old girl. She was on holiday with her parents in a hired cabin cruiser and one of her proud duties was to assist in manoeuvring it through the locks. It was while tying up to one of the posts, at the entrance to Temple Lock, that she made her discovery and it might have passed her by altogether if an excess of zeal had not caused her to lose her balance at the crucial moment and obliged her to fling both arms round the post for support. In doing so she knocked her plastic sunglasses off and they fell into the water. As soon as order was restored and the rope made fast, she had leant out as far as she could, sideways over the stern, in a futile attempt to retrieve them. They had floated tantalisingly a few inches beyond her reach and were bobbing gracefully along towards a clump of weeds just below the surface, between the post and the weir. She was studying the terrain and assessing the chances of their being caught and held there long enough for her to get the boat hook into position when she saw the tip of a man's grey and sodden shoe. It was not floating on the water, but sticking straight up through the weeds, and being a fast-thinking girl she immediately lost interest in the glasses and went forward to the steering cabin to tell her father.

These facts only came to my notice later on, for all Robin would say when he telephoned me after lunch at Toby's was that Mike's body had been pulled out of the river and was now at the morgue awaiting a post mortem.

"You look rather disappointed," Toby remarked when I had passed on the news. "But I suppose you could call it a happy ending in one respect."

"For Chloe maybe, but not for Brenda. She was fighting mad when she thought he'd bolted with another woman, but all the stuffing will go out of her now. My guess is that she'll spend the rest of her life wondering what made him do it and how she'd let him down."

"I can't help wondering a bit myself."

"Nor can I. Do you suppose it had anything to do with the way he'd mucked things up for Chloe? It would have been a bad blow to his self-esteem, if nothing else."

"Oh no, I can't agree. These fantasy fairy godfathers can always put their failures behind them and dance on to the next good deed."

"Then what reason can you suggest?"

"I daresay he didn't have one. He was probably a little overwrought and fell in by mistake."

"In broad daylight? Surely somebody would have fished him out?"

"How do you know it was broad daylight?"

"Because he disappeared between eight-thirty and nine-thirty in the morning."

"But he needn't necessarily have plunged straight in. He could have been on a blind somewhere first and finished up at night in the pub where they found his car. What more natural, when closing time came, to go for a stroll to clear his head before driving home? I can picture it all: the weaving gait as he lurches towards the river, the fatal stumble, the faint splash and smothered scream, before the waters close over his head."

"You may be able to picture it like that, Toby, but I certainly can't. For one thing, as I've told you so many times already, he never touched a drop."

"How can you be sure of that? Just think of all the new and wonderful things you've learnt about him only this morning! However, I've got something else for you; how do you like the idea of his wife having pushed him in?"

"Same objection. How could she have done so without anyone noticing? At this time of the year the Thames is like Oxford Street a week before Christmas, as you well know. Besides . . ."

"Yes?"

"Well, Robin probably wouldn't have any truck with this, but I honestly can't see what her motive would have been. I daresay being married to Mike was a lonely and boring occupation for much of the time, but it's going to be far more lonely and boring without him and obviously there were compensations. She was well provided for and living in her dream house and I expect all that will come to an end now. He may have been earning quite a lot recently, but people in our business hardly ever manage to save much, do they? Whatever his faults, and he does seem to have had a few which didn't meet the naked eye, she can hardly fail to be worse off without him."

"I'm not sure that I'll have any truck with that either," Toby said. "One never really knows anything about people's circumstances except what they choose to reveal. For all you know, she may have another Mister in the background, all ready to take over the mortgage and the marriage bed."

"You wouldn't get that impression if you met her; but in any case there's a much more factual objection."

"I look forward to hearing it."

"Several, in fact. I've already pointed out the obstacles confronting a woman desirous of pushing her husband into the Thames at the height of the holiday season, and before you tell me that she could have enticed him to some secluded spot and by some miracle hit on a moment when there was no one in sight, I must tell you that she simply could not have had the opportunity."

"Oh, how can you say so? She has given you her version of how she spent the day, but naturally she would have left out that bit."

"No, that's the whole point, Toby. If the version she gave me was fictitious, why did she drag in so many details which could be checked? She lived such a tame, uneventful life that it would have been impossible to prove she was lying if she had described a day in which nothing whatever happened, not even a visit to the supermarket or the man coming to check the electric meter. Furthermore, why bring her story to me at all? If she had pushed him in, surely the sensible course would have been to lie low and hope that he would never turn up at all or that when he did he'd be unrecognisable?"

"Because it might appear slightly callous, in the circumstances to say nothing about it and go quietly plodding on with the housework, as though one husband more or less made no difference."

"In most households that might apply, I agree, but not to Brenda. She could always have stuck to her story that Mike had told her he had to be away on location. It's not a very likely thing to happen, but masses of people would have confirmed that she was in no position to know that. They all tell the same story about his keeping her completely in the dark, so far as his work was concerned, and of using it as an excuse for his neglect."

"In that case, what about the other one?"

"Chloe?"

"She appears to have had quite a sound motive."

"Too sound by half. I mean, she'd hardly have confessed to it so openly if she was guilty, do you think?"

"Who knows? Blabbing away to comparative strangers is reputed to be quite a common failing among criminals. I daresay very few of them would ever be caught if they only knew how to exercise a little self-control."

"Don't let Robin hear you say that; and anyway I doubt if Chloe is the type to fall into that sort of trap. She's a very cool number. On the other hand, let's say for the sake of argument that Mike turned up at her cottage, all set to tangle her life yet again and she decided she'd had enough. She could have pretended to be willing to discuss whatever he had in mind, but not where her brother might overhear. It would have been the most natural thing in the world to have suggested taking a stroll along the towpath. In fact, it's about the only place round there where you could take a stroll. She's a fairly powerful girl, quite as strong as Mike I should imagine, and if she'd had the forethought to conceal a brick about her person, she could have knocked him out and heaved him in with no trouble at all."

"Without anyone seeing? How would that apply to her and not to the wife?"

"Because of the lock. During the ten minutes or so when the gates are closed, all the craft coming down-stream would have been completely sealed off. She'd only have needed to watch for anything approaching from the other direction and they'd be travelling slowly, getting ready to wait their turn to go in."

"There you are, then. There's your case all sewn up. Having thrown him into the water, she drives his car to the Strand, leaves it near the pub and then goes home to bed."

"How?"

"Well, in the usual way, I suppose . . . draw back the bedclothes . . . one two three, jump?"

"I meant how did she get home? No car, remember, and it must be at least fifteen miles by road. No, I am sorry to say, Toby, that whether Chloe killed him or not, she couldn't have done it in the way I've described."

"Oh, what a pity! I feel quite cheated."

"So do I, but the trouble is I'd overlooked his car, and, what is much worse, I'd forgotten about the current. Chloe's cottage is between Cookham and Marlow, but Temple Lock, where Mike was found, is a long way upstream from there. Wherever he was put into the river, he must either have remained in that spot, or been pulled along the current. By no stretch of the imagination could he have drifted against it. I can guess what you're going to say next."

"Well that's lucky, because I can't."

"You could have said that, instead of walking, Chloe and Mike went for a drive somewhere, having locked her brother in the cottage, that she killed him in some secluded spot just above Temple Lock, drove his car to the Strand and paddled herself home in a stolen punt."

"And what is your objection to this brilliant exposition of mine?"

"First of all that the boatman at the Strand hasn't reported a missing punt; only a missing pole."

"Oh well, no one is infallible. He may not have noticed."

"Surely he would have noticed if someone had pinched one of his punts in broad daylight? It could only have been done after dark, when he had gone home."

"Quite so."

I shook my head: "Not so at all. You see, all the locks are closed at sunset, so she couldn't have gone more than a few miles by river. The only remaining alternative is that they met by arrangement at the pub, she having left her own car somewhere nearby, but that's not really feasible either. I simply cannot see them sitting side by side in his car until well past closing time when the whole area is deserted, at which point he allows her to conk him on the head and drag him off down to the river. No, it's too ridiculous to contemplate and I am afraid the answer has to be suicide. I do wonder why he did it, though?"

"There could be a thousand reasons. Obviously he wasn't quite the simple soul you took him for."

"No, but he had his good points too, whatever Chloe may say, and it's sad to think of him ending his life so drearily. Rough on the boys too, when they learn the truth."

"Your sentiments do you credit, but I shouldn't lose a moment's sleep over the last one. If you can't puzzle out why he did it, I see no reason why any coroner should. It will be put down to accidental death."

"Yes, I hadn't thought of it, but you're probably right. It's a consoling thought."

A short lived one too, as it turned out, for less than twenty-four hours had passed when Robin gave me the result of the autopsy and it established conclusively that death had not been caused by drowning. I suspected that even the most charitable coroner might have some trouble in postulating that a man could have accidentally fallen into the river, having first accidentally suffocated himself to death.

"Wheels within wheels," Toby remarked, when I telephoned the news, for he likes to be kept abreast of events, so long as he is not required to play any active part in them. "You mark my words!"

I wish I had too, because as things turned out he was so absolutely right.

CHAPTER TEN

SYMPATHY with Brenda's ordeal in identifying her husband's remains, plus the inability to expunge the disagreeable images it created, prompted me to make several attempts to ring her up. The first was at half past nine in the morning, but there was no reply and, concluding that she was doing some shopping after seeing the children on to the school bus, I waited for an hour before trying again. Still no reply, either then, or on my third attempt just before lunch. It had occurred to me by then that her number might be out of order, so I enlisted the operator's help. However, this got me nowhere because after a few whirrs and clicks I was back with the ringing tone again. Whereupon she informed me that my number was ringing for me now, and disappeared into the ether before I could comment.

There is nothing to compare with such little bureaucratic pinpricks for setting one off on a defiant course, however ill-advised, and I had gathered up my bag and keys and marched out of the house within three minutes of putting the receiver down and certainly without stopping to consider what I might be letting myself in for.

The answer to that one appeared, initially, to be a forty mile drive with nothing whatever at the end of it, for when I pulled up outside 32, Hill Grove, I saw a young woman walking slowly away from the house, wheeling a wispy, flaxen-haired tot in a pushchair. Reaching the gate as I alighted, she first shook her head at me and then turned it away to glance back at the house.

She herself was a waif-like creature, heavily pregnant, wearing a pale blue smock and flat-soled leather sandals. Her head was tied up in a chiffon scarf, which failed to camouflage the lumps and bumps of hair rollers underneath, and she looked weary as well as anxious.

"No one at home?" I asked her.

"I guess that's what we're meant to think, only it isn't true. She's in there, I'd say, and so are the kids. Trouble is, she refuses to open up. My name's Fay Burnett, by the way," she added, holding out her hand.

"How do you do? I'm Tessa Price."

"Nice to meet you. Haven't I seen you before?"

"On the screen, possibly. Calling myself Theresa Crichton."

"Oh, sure, I remember now. I heard you on the radio only the other day. You a friend of Mrs Parsons?"

"Not really. I knew her husband fairly well."

"Then you've heard what happened? Him being drowned, I mean?"

"It's why I've come. Not much use though, if she won't let me in. Are you quite sure she's there?"

"She has to be. The boys didn't get the bus this morning and she doesn't have a car now. Besides, I lifted the letter box flap to try and take a look inside and I could hear people moving around. She's always like this, did you know? I've been around to call on her several times, but she won't open the door. Hell, I don't know why I bother, but it's on account of the kids mainly. I've got three of my own, in addition to number four due next month. This one is Claire, by the way. Say hello to Mrs Price, Claire."

"Hello, Claire!"

"You know, I just can't stop myself worrying about Mrs Parsons shut up in there on her own. One shouldn't repeat things, but you were a friend of his, and from what I hear she has this drinking problem . . . did you know about that?"

"I've heard rumours, but I wouldn't let it worry you too much. Personally, I think they're exaggerated. Anyway, you shouldn't be standing about like this. Can't I give you a lift home?"

"No, it's okay. We only live just a way up the hill a bit."

"Really? I'd guessed that you came from much further off."

"Oh, you mean my accent? Well yes, I'm American and I guess it shows. Drew, that's my husband, is in the U.S. Air Force."

"How long have you been here?"

"Only four, five months. Seems a whole lot longer sometimes," she added wistfully.

"Is that all?" I asked.

"What's so surprising?"

"That it should be a newcomer like yourself who bothers about one of the neighbours. Especially as I gather Mrs Parsons is hell bent on keeping herself to herself."

"Is she ever? But her husband wasn't at all like that, was he? He was real nice to us when we first moved in here. It was wonderful really because we'd had it well beaten into us how difficult it was to establish any kind of relationships with the British, and the rest of the neighbours certainly acted pretty snooty. But Mike was different. He went out of his way to help us all he could and he and Drew got to be real good friends in the end. That's why when I heard what people around here were saying, I felt I owed it to Mike to take a hand."

"What are they saying?"

"Oh, you know; about her being an alcoholic and keeping the place like a pigsty, so that he had to set to and clean it up himself very often. So they're not surprised he couldn't take any more and did himself in. That's what they call it. It didn't seem right, somehow, just to put all the blame on her and forget about it. Not that I've done any good."

"All the same, it was kind of you to try. Are you sure you don't want a lift? That pushchair will easily fit in the boot."

"No, I'll be fine. Maybe you should see what you can do with Mrs Parsons. And I hope you have more luck than I did. Bye for now, it's been nice meeting you."

Contrary to expectations, her hope was realised, for the bell had hardly whispered its first chime than the front door was pulled aside, just far enough to reveal Barry's head and shoulders.

"Mum wants to see you," he announced.

"It's mutual, but you'll have to open up a little wider than that if I'm to get through."

Reluctantly, he gave me an inch or two more, then slammed the door shut again as soon as I had squeezed past. Drink-sodden slattern or not, Brenda certainly had her children squarely under her thumb.

She was seated in an armchair, apparently staring at one of the cream walls, although it was impossible even to be sure that her eyes were open, for she had retreated behind the sunglasses again. Nevertheless, she greeted me in a fairly steady voice and the mystery of her gruesome reputation remained unsolved, although a tentative explanation for it now began to take shape somewhere at the back of my mind.

"Has she gone?" Brenda demanded.

"Who?"

"That American creature who was snooping around here."

"Yes, she's gone. I think she only wanted to help, you know."

"I can do without her help, thank you very much. I've no time for people like that. All I want is to be left alone."

In view of her implacable hostility to almost everyone around her, I did not consider this requirement to be over-ambitious and I said:

"Does that include me?"

"No, you're different. More of an outsider, as you might say. Besides, it was me who came to you in the first place. I wouldn't have done that if I'd known he was dead all the time. There wouldn't have been any point, would there? But it never entered my head he'd do such a thing. I still can't bring myself to believe it. Him killing himself, I mean."

Since it was not an idea she would need to adjust to for very long, I ignored this and passed on to a more practical problem:

"I'm afraid there may be something wrong with your telephone. Naturally, I wouldn't have chosen to burst in on you like this without warning, but the trouble is that it sounds as though your bell was ringing, but obviously you don't hear it."

"Oh yes I do."

"You mean you're purposely not answering it? That did occur to me too, but why, Brenda? What's the point of barricading yourself like this?"

"I'm not. I let you in, didn't I?"

"Yes, but what's wrong with answering the telephone? It couldn't possibly do any harm."

"That's what you think," she retorted, removing the glasses at last, although perhaps only because they had become so misted with tears that she could no longer see, for, keeping her head lowered, she began scrubbing away at the lenses with the hem of her dress.

"What are you afraid of, Brenda?"

"I've been getting anonymous phone calls, if you must know."

"Who from?" I asked, then seeing the inanity of the question amended it to:

"Man or woman?"

"Both."

"Oh come now, you're not seriously suggesting they're a team?"

"I don't know who they are, or how many of them. I don't know what it is they're trying to do either, and that's what frightens me. It's as though I was surrounded by all these enemies and I've no idea who they are or what I've done to make them hate me so."

"Aren't you dramatising it a bit? I mean, what did they say exactly? Can you remember?"

"The first time they didn't say anything at all. It was about three o'clock in the morning. Day before yesterday. It woke me up and I lay there in a sort of daze, hearing it ring. It went on and on and then it dawned on me that the only person who could be phoning at that hour was Mike. This was before they told me he was dead, you see. So I tore out of bed and downstairs to the hall to answer it."

"And?"

"Nothing. I kept saying: 'Hello! Who's there?' but no one spoke. Just this kind of heavy breathing, like you hear about."

"So you hung up?"

"No, I couldn't bring myself to. I was still clinging to this mad idea that it must be Mike. I know it sounds silly, but he did sometimes play practical jokes, and I didn't realise at the time how late it was. I'd gone to bed early and I hadn't stopped to look at my watch when the phone went, so it might not have been more than eleven or so. But then, just as I was getting desperate, this caller, whoever he was, gave a kind of giggle and rang off. It made me feel really ill, I can tell you."

"And looking back on it, do you still believe it was a man?"

"Couldn't say, but it wasn't Mike, that I do know. I've never heard him laugh like that."

"What about the next time?"

"That was only a few hours later. I hadn't managed to get off to sleep again and in the end I got up and went out to the garden, thinking a breath of air might calm me down. I was on my way back indoors again to make myself a cup of tea and just as I got to the patio the phone rang again. I nearly jumped out of my skin. I was too frightened even to move at first, but it went on and on, just like the first time and I was afraid one of the boys might hear it and come down, so I forced myself to go inside and pick it up."

"What happened? Same thing again?"

"Oh no, this time it was some woman. She started talking as soon as I lifted the receiver, but I couldn't take anything in at first. There was something about how she'd heard the news and wanted to warn me before the papers came. It was all pouring out of her so fast that I couldn't get a word in edgeways, but at last I managed to say that I didn't understand what she was talking about and then she turned very sharp all of a sudden. She kept repeating, 'Who is this? Who is this?' in a sort of cross way, and I couldn't make that out either. It was as though she was asking me to say who she was, instead of the other way round. In the end it turned out she'd got the wrong number. It wasn't even the same exchange as ours. Or at any rate, that's what she pretended."

"And it could have been true, you know. I can understand how the two calls coming on top of each other must have been unnerving for you, but it sounds to me like a very unlucky coincidence. The first one was probably some drunk who thought it would be amusing to pick out a few numbers at random and give people a scare, and the second could easily have been a wrong number, as she said. I daresay you wouldn't have given it a thought in normal times."

"But these aren't normal times, are they? And it's all tied up with Mike's death in some way, I'm convinced of it. You haven't heard about the third call yet."

"No, when was that?"

"Soon after nine. I'd just got back from taking the boys down to the bus. It was a man's voice that time, and he didn't ask me who I was or anything like that. He just said: 'Mike's dead, you know, so that makes you a murderess! How do you like that?' Or it may have been: 'How do you care for that?' I was so shocked I can't remember exactly. Anyway, since then I haven't dared answer the phone at all."

"Let me get this straight, Brenda. You said this call came through yesterday, soon after nine, but wasn't that before you, or anyone else except the police knew that Mike was dead?"

"That's right, it was getting on for lunch time when they brought me the news. They were very kind, you know, and sympathetic. Made it all sound like I would be doing them a great favour if I'd go with them to the mortuary and identify him, but I could see that it would be a fat lot of use to refuse. They said it would only take a minute and that part was true, but it's not a minute I'm likely to forget in a hurry."

"No, I can imagine. Did you tell the police about these calls?"

"No."

"Not even the last one?"

"I was too upset about Mike to remember anything else. And they didn't ask me any questions. Only things like whether there were any friends or relations I'd like them to notify; or whether there was some neighbour they could ask to come over and sit with me for a bit. I gave them Mike's parents' address in New Zealand. That's where he came from, you know, and I've never set eyes on them. My own are both dead, but I've got a sister living up North and I rang her myself. She and her husband are coming down for the funeral. And I certainly don't want any of the neighbours poking their noses in. The less I see of that lot the better. That's why I kept the boys home from school today."

"You won't be able to keep that up indefinitely."

"I know, but it'll be their holidays soon and my sister did offer to have us up to stay with them for a week or two. She didn't sound too pressing about it, but I suppose she thought it would look funny if she didn't invite us. Her husband's done quite well for himself and they've got a biggish place near Halifax, so it isn't much trouble for her."

"Then I should certainly go. It might do you good to get away for a bit," I said, reflecting that it might also do me good if she were to get away for a bit.

"Of course I shan't be able to leave until after the funeral, and then there'll be the inquest. What's likely to happen there, do you know?"

This was dangerous ground and I gave her a vague answer, which luckily seemed to satisfy her and then, to push the subject still further into the background, I said:

"By the way, to go back to that last telephone call, you didn't by any chance get a clue as to who it might have been?"

Brenda sighed deeply: "I've been thinking about it ever such a lot, but the trouble is the more I go back over it the harder it is to remember what I thought at the time and what I've imagined since. I suppose that's partly why I didn't mention it to the police. I knew I'd get all tied up in knots and start contradicting myself, so where would be the use?"

"That rather sounds as though you did recognise him?"

"Yes. Mind you, I only heard his voice once before, but he sounded to me like the one who called himself Sandy. You remember I told you about him ringing up on the morning Mike disappeared."

"Yes, I do, and it reminds me that no one at A.I.P. seems to know him. I asked several people when I was there the other day."

"Well, there you are then! What's the point of saying anything to the police?"

"Although presumably it could be a special nick-name which only his closest friends call him by? That's a thought, isn't it?"

"Oh, what's it matter, anyway?" Brenda asked impatiently. "It's over and done with now and finding out who this Sandy is won't bring Mike back, or help me to understand why he killed himself."

The conversation had taken another dangerous turn and mistrusting my discretion to last out indefinitely, I made an excuse to leave, reminding her to let me know if she ever wanted my help.

"Don't get up," I added. "I'll see myself out."

Most likely the offer was superfluous, for she had folded back into inertia again and my last image of her was of the white face behind the dense black circles, staring at nothing.

There was a smart blue van parked in the lane, with *Briggs & Cox. Provisions, Wines Spirits* painted in gold letters on its side, and as I was getting into my car a small, grim-faced young man with a red beard emerged from the back of it, staggering under the weight of a brown cardboard box.

"You going out, Missus?" he called.

"Not exactly. I don't live here, as it happens."

"Sorry, dear! Seeing you from the back I took you for the lady of the house. She in?"

"Yes, but she may not open the door to you. There's been some trouble in the family and she's not feeling well."

"Wouldn't surprise me," he answered laconically. "Only I still got to get this lot signed for, if they want me to leave it."

"What's in it, anyway?" I asked, moving closer to the box, which he had now slid on to the bonnet of his van.

It was divided into a dozen compartments, each one containing a bottle. There were six of whisky and six of gin.

"Can't see me leaving that lot without a signature, can you?"

"I should think there must be some mistake, though. Are you sure these were ordered?"

"Name of Parsons?"

"That's right."

"No mistake then, dear. Got it all down here, if you want to look. Parsons. Number 32. Standing Order. Account number 5401. Anything wrong with that?"

I was half inclined to warn him that account number 5401 might now be closed, but he was not such an endearing character as to make me eager to save him trouble, and, furthermore, there was always the chance that I was wrong.

CHAPTER ELEVEN

"To change to a less controversial subject," Robin said to me at dinner that evening. "What can you tell us about this mysterious Sandy?"

The 'us' in this context referred to himself and Toby, the latter having driven to London with me after my call at Hill Grove, in order to dine and spend the night at Beacon Square. He and I were the possessors of coveted tickets for a memorial service at St Martins-in-the-Fields the following morning to mark the passing, a few weeks earlier, of a distinguished actor manager. Speculation round the dinner table regarding this gala occasion had led to an acrimonious argument about the longevity of so many members of the profession, a subject on which we all held positive but widely differing views, and Robin's request had probably been inspired more by a desire to end the resulting belligerent stalemate than from genuine curiosity.

"Why? Do you think he may be important?" I asked, nevertheless clutching at this rare opportunity to enlist his interest in the case of Mike Parsons.

"I wouldn't go as far as that. I am just faintly puzzled by the fact that your new friend, Brenda, had apparently never heard of him until her husband went missing, after which he rarely seems to be off the telephone."

"What's puzzling about that? Presumably, he's someone who worked with Mike at the studios and there wouldn't have been any occasion to enquire for him at home until he disappeared. It's true that of all the people I've asked only Chloe had vaguely heard of him, but what does that prove? The sound department is a little ivory tower all on its own and it was probably simply a case of asking the wrong people."

"Or the wrong questions?" Robin suggested.

"What were the right ones?"

"Well, to start with, are you certain that Sandy is a man?"

"I don't see what else he could be."

"Admittedly it's a name one associates with that sex rather than the other, and perhaps Brenda did so automatically, but it isn't always so. I once knew a model called Sandy, although I believe her real name was Sandra."

"Is that so?" I asked. "You never told me about her."

"There was no reason to. It all happened years before I met you."

"All what happened?"

"Nothing. Figure of speech."

"Where is she now?"

"How would I know? I keep telling you, I lost touch with her years ago."

"What a pity!" Toby said, intervening at this point. "If she has a deep, masculine voice and speaks with an American accent, she could be the very one we're looking for."

"Why American?" Robin asked sharply.

"Isn't that what you said, Tessa?"

"Yes," I replied, "I seem to remember Brenda telling me so. Does it have any significance?"

"Probably not, although, funnily enough, among the odds and ends they found in the abandoned car there was a book on wild birds. It was an American edition, not for sale over here, so presumably it was lent or given to him by someone."

"No 'love from Sandy' on the flyleaf?" Toby enquired.

"Not so far as I know, and I daresay there's no connection whatever. After all, there must be quite a number of Americans around in the film industry."

"And not only there!"

"That's quite true," I agreed, struck by another memory, but before I could put it into words Toby asked: "What else did they find in the car?"

"Nothing very helpful. I made a list, in case Tessa was interested, but after all she doesn't seem to be."

"I've been pursuing other trails," I explained, "but I'd love to hear your list, if you've still got it."

Robin brought a note book out of his breast pocket and, after a brief search, began to read aloud:

"One tweed jacket, well worn, two buttons missing, one found in right hand pocket. Nothing else in pockets. Several maps and manuals in the glove compartment, also current A.A. book, log book and insurance certificate; plus highway code and the usual assortment that you find in most family cars, i.e. paper handkerchiefs, half full tin of butterscotch, pair of black gloves, female; spectacle case, empty. There was mud and gravel under and around the seats, leaves and twigs in the luggage compartment at the back. Also in the back compartment traces of wheelmarks. The last two items caused some mystification, but Tessa already had the explanation for one of them, which Mrs Parsons endorsed, and she was also able to account for the second. It seems that when the family went out for an excursion they often took the boys' bikes along with them in the back of the car."

"And that was all?" I asked.

"Yes. Nothing very sensational, I'm afraid."

"On the contrary, I find it full of interest. As much for what it leaves out as for what it includes."

"Is that so? And what does it leave out?"

I had been thinking mainly of the missing three hundred pounds, but there was another item tucked away in Robin's list which had set up an entirely new train of thought and I said:

"I'm not sure yet. I'll need time to think about it."

Robin and Toby thereupon exchanged what I understand are called meaningful glances and Toby murmured that some actors might retain their youthful powers to a very great age, whereas others, it appeared, became senile in their twenties.

"Which could be one reason for living on as they do," Robin submitted. "Not wearing themselves out with mental exertion, they have that much more vitality to spare than the rest of us."

This unkind judgement brought us round in full circle and the subject of Mike Parsons' death was temporarily shelved.

*

The memorial service proved to be an impressive occasion, with hardly a dry eye in the congregation. All the women were dressed as for a dull day at Ascot and there was a full quorum of knights and dames. Press and television cameramen thronged the steps and pavement and it was quite a surprise not to see the House Full boards propped against the pillars. Certainly there was hardly an empty seat in the church and it was only by resorting to trickery that Toby managed to snatch one on the aisle, which happens to rank among the prime essentials of his life.

The trickery in question consisted of shoving me ahead of him into a pew which was virtually full, and so obliging the other occupants to shuffle up one by one, like a line of soldiers closing ranks. They did not look particularly cheerful about this, but luckily the poor sufferer who found himself wedged up against me turned out to be my old friend, Peter Bliss the film director, and his outraged glare mellowed a little when he saw who it was under the brown straw hat. By the end of the service, which had us both in tears, his last defences were down and he invited me to take a restorative gin and tonic. The amnesty did not extend to Toby however, which I was glad about for there were one or two searching questions of a confidential nature which I wished to put to Peter concerning the line up of future productions, if any, at A.I.P.

That the winds from this quarter were unfavourable was evinced from the start by the fact that instead of taking me to the Savoy, as I had confidently expected, he grasped my arm and marched me briskly off in the opposite direction. We landed up some five minutes later in a rather dingy pub off St Martin's Lane, which had puddles of beer on all the tables and where the ashtrays were no doubt emptied with the utmost regularity once a fortnight.

Nor was the tenor of our conversation any more heartening, for according to Peter the native film industry was now practically in its death throes. The producers had pared down the budget on his current film to a record breaking, laughable low, the so-called star rarely if ever drew a sober breath, and he was strongly of the opinion that he personally would never be invited to direct another picture.

Altogether, it gave every indication of going into the files as the most wasted forty minutes of my life, but luckily things brightened up a bit when we moved into the realms of rumour and speculation and Peter provided at least one morsel of more than passing interest. This came when he said:

"You remember Alec?"

"Ferguson? Yes, of course."

"You've heard he's no longer with us?"

"No. Do you mean he's dead?"

Peter laughed. "How readily your tiny mind leaps to such conclusions! It must be the company you keep."

"Not at all. People often do use that kind of euphemism when they mean someone has died, and furthermore one of Alec's colleagues was picked out of the river a few days ago, as you may have heard, so one is naturally influenced towards that line of thought."

"Oh, indeed!" Peter agreed. "Perhaps rather more naturally than you realise. The grapevine has it that there is some connection."

"Why? And what exactly happened to Alec? What does 'no longer with us' actually mean?"

"What it says; that he's alive, though not very well, and living in Pinner, having voted himself three months' unpaid leave on account of a slipped disc."

"Oh, how dull! Your silly old grapevine must have been stretched to the limits to make anything out of that. I was hoping for something much more sensational."

"Then you shall have it, darling. The gossips say he's actually on the edge of a nervous breakdown."

"Well yes, that's a bit more like it; and I can see that if it were true he might prefer to put it about that it was a disc rather than the other thing, especially if he wants his job kept open."

"It hasn't occurred to you to wonder why Alec, of all our solid citizens, should be suffering from a nervous breakdown?"

"No, I can't say it had. There could be all sorts of reasons, couldn't there? I mean, it must be a fairly demanding job."

"Honestly, Tessa, what will you say next? He and Sally ran that department like two old ladies knitting up the parish accounts at Little Middling in the Marsh. Even getting the daily call sheets out of them was like asking for the moon."

"All the same, he had a lot of responsibility. That can be wearing."

"My darling girl, you're talking the most arrant piffle. Haven't I been sitting here laboriously spelling out the catastrophic situation we all find ourselves in? Can't I get it through to you that anyone who is blessed with a safe job wouldn't willingly give it up, even on his death-bed? If anyone has his big feet firmly on the ground it's Alec and he must see that this could easily finish him, so far as A.I.P. is concerned. The chances of getting his job back at the end of three months are such as you would not readily spot under a powerful microscope."

"All right, then, so what has your precious old grape-vine come up with? That Alec hounded Mike Parsons to his death and is now so shaken by remorse that he dare not show his face in public?"

Peter looked at me thoughtfully. "Move up to the top of the class."

"Oh, honestly! Who's joking now? I didn't mean that seriously."

"No? Then it's a remarkable coincidence that you got so close to the mark. It was Sally who told me. She's running the office temporarily until they get a replacement for Alec so I have to see quite a lot of her, one way and another, and yesterday evening she broke down and confessed all. She's a bit thrown, I must tell you, because naturally she's all on Alec's side and it bothers her to think of him suffering in such an unworthy cause."

"The unworthy cause being Mike?"

"Right. According to her, Alec had been covering up for him for months. He was invariably late on the job, or left early and sometimes didn't turn up at all. He always made the same excuse and Alec always fell for it. Until recently, that is."

"Don't tell me," I begged. "Let me guess! The excuse for this erratic behaviour was that his wife was an alcoholic and that in addition to his job he had to take care of her and very often the children and the housework as well?"

"So you know all about it," Peter said crossly. "Why do I bother?"

"No, I didn't know, but it wasn't a particularly inspired guess because it ties up with other things I've heard. Tell me this, though: what happened to make Alec change his mind?"

"Did I say so?"

"It amounted to that. You said that he had always fallen for these excuses until recently. Suggesting that he finally saw through them."

"Oh, that was just my slovenly way of speaking. The impression I got from Sally was that he had never ceased to believe implicitly in Mike, which is precisely why he is feeling so wretched about it now. Apparently, what happened recently was that he'd told Mike he was very sorry for him and all that, and if it was up to him he'd play along indefinitely, but with all the pressures on him just now and the front office breathing down his neck he simply couldn't cover up any longer. Either Mike would have to make some arrangement for his wife, like putting her in a home or whatever, or else he'd be for the chopper. It seems Mike told him they'd already tried a cure, but it hadn't worked, so Alec said 'Well, too bad', or words to that effect, and Sally believes he's now convinced that this was the last straw which drove Mike to suicide. Naturally, he doesn't feel too hilarious about it."

"No, but do you really mean he expects it to take him three months moping in Pinner to get over it? I thought Alec was made of sterner stuff than that."

"Oh well, you know what some of these Scots are? Alec has a tough exterior, but there's a mass of sentiment gurgling away underneath. And he had rather a thing about that Mike. No, I don't mean what you mean. It was more a terrible kind of Barrie thing really. He has no children, so he probably saw him as the baby son who never was. However, one mustn't be bitchy because it can't be nice to live with the knowledge that he was the one to send Mike to his death, as it were."

"I don't think that's at all as it were. For one thing," I began, and then, since this conversation was taking place before the true cause of death had been made known, I stopped short and attacked the subject from a different direction. "For one thing, not many sons tell their fathers the whole truth and I daresay Mike was no exception. He was a much more complicated character than any of us realised and he operated on several different levels, with a matching face for each of them. For what it's worth, you can tell Sally from me that Alec has nothing whatever to reproach himself for."

"I shouldn't imagine it would even be worth the trip down to her office, and frankly, Tessa, it astonishes me that you should profess to know Mike better than Alec did. He can hardly have been more to you than someone you occasionally ran across at the studios."

"A little more than that, as it happens, but what matters is that I've come to know him rather better since his death. I can't tell you how."

"Why not?"

"Because it would involve several other people who've told me things in confidence."

"Well, if you're going to play it so mysterious, I can't see how you can expect anyone to take you seriously."

"Nor do I, really. Not that it signifies. You'll see that I was right before many days are out."

"Oh, my darling Cassandra, I don't believe a word of it. Do you want another drink? No, on second thoughts, I must leave you now, I've got a lunch date. Which way are you going?"

"Home. It's all right, I'll find a cab. Thanks a lot."

"Yer welcome!" he said, stressing the American accent.

It reminded me of something and when we were out in the street, scanning the horizon for empty taxis, I said: "By the way, Pete, what's Alec's full name?"

"Ferguson."

"No, I didn't mean that. I was wondering if Alec was short for Alexander."

"Why not? That's usual, isn't it?"

"Yes, I believe it is."

"More mysteries?"

"No, it just occurred to me that there's another way of shortening Alexander, isn't there?"

I cannot be sure that he heard this, for he had stepped off the pavement as I spoke and was now gyrating about and snapping his fingers like a pop singer in full cry, as two cruising taxis approached. He did give me rather an enquiring look as he turned, with his hand on the door of the first one, but already regretting having uttered my thoughts aloud I waved goodbye and launched myself at the second.

CHAPTER TWELVE

NOT unexpectedly, it was the medical evidence which provided the big sensation at Mike Parsons' inquest and the verdict, inevitably, was Murder by Person or Persons Unknown.

Having been prepared, unlike most of those present, for these two bombshells, I was able to spare the greater part of my attention for my surroundings, which contained one or two interesting features. Brenda was in court, but her testimony was read aloud and she was not called upon to go into the box. Also she was wearing the black goggles, so it was impossible to tell how much the surgeon's evidence came as a shock to her and whether she had known in advance that her husband had been suffocated and was dead when he entered the water.

She was accompanied by a middle-aged couple, both in mourning, of whom the female, although stouter and more opulent looking, bore sufficient resemblance to her to make it certain that she was the sister from Halifax. Considering their presence to provide all that was necessary in moral support, I kept well away and seated myself with a handful of other spectators at the back of the court-room. None of these, to the best of my knowledge, were from A.I.P. and, except in one case, it was not possible to tell whether they included representatives from Hill Grove. The single exception was a sallow, sharp featured and slight young man in the uniform of a U.S. Air Force sergeant, seated in the row ahead of mine, but to one side, so that I had a clear view of his left profile. It availed me nothing, however, for he chewed gum throughout the proceedings, causing me to make a mental note of the fact that this is the most effective device of all for concealing emotions, superior even to sunglasses.

Otherwise, from my point of view, there was only one unforeseen development and it came from the coroner's request for a description of the deceased's clothing when he was taken out of the river. A police detective listed it as follows: dark blue cotton trousers, blue and white shirt; no tie, dark blue blazer with metal buttons, white or cream socks, canvas shoes.

I was still pondering over these particulars when the hearing broke up and in consequence was not sufficiently quick off the mark in making for the exit. The Air Force sergeant beat me to the door and by the time I reached it the way was blocked by two stout, slow moving females. In the few seconds it took me to squeeze and apologise my way past them my quarry contrived to vanish altogether. Peering around for a likely looking car, I was waylaid by Brenda, who broke away from her protective guard to approach me, although at first too shaken by sobs to utter a single word.

"I'm so sorry," I said. "It must have been a hideous shock for you."

"No, it wasn't," she mumbled, managing to control herself a little. "They told me about it yesterday; but they won't tell me anything else. They won't say who they think did it."

"Well no, it's a bit early for that, but they're bound to find out in time."

"No, they won't. How could they? Who could possibly want to do such a horrible thing? Can you think of anyone?"

It was hardly the moment to do justice to such a question and also I could see the sister and brother-in-law fidgeting impatiently in the background, so I said:

"Listen, Brenda, let's talk about it some other time. I think you ought to go home now and rest for a bit."

"But you will come and see me? Say you will? You're about the only person I can speak my mind to. Can you come tomorrow?"

"I thought you were going to stay with your sister?"

"No, the police say I've to stop on here for a few days. They say there'll be things they have to ask me. Everything's changed now, you see, from what we thought."

"But can't your sister stay here with you?"

"Not her! She's as selfish as they come. Still, they have offered to take Barry and Keith up north with them. It's best like that and I'd really rather be on my own, specially if I know I can always get in touch with you, if I need to. Well, I'd better go now, or they'll start fussing, but give me a ring, will you?"

"Will you answer if I do?"

"Yes. The superintendent told me I must. I mentioned about those calls, like you told me to, and he's going to have the line tapped. So what I've got to do if I get any more of them is to try to give them a chance to trace where he's speaking from. And I shan't feel so afraid when I know they're listening in."

I was tempted to remind her that this clever scheme was likely to fall flat on its face if she continued to broadcast the details on the public highway, but I could see that the selfish sister's patience was rapidly running out, so having promised Brenda to telephone her between nine and ten the following morning, I made my escape.

CHAPTER THIRTEEN

IT WAS a fortunate chance which had limited the invitations to the party for our fictitious wedding anniversary to only two people, for both of whom it provided a ready made excuse for further communication, and I started as usual with the nut which I anticipated being the harder of these to crack.

Rejecting the telephone for once in my life, nevertheless my first move was to consult the directory. There were numerous A. Fergusons listed, but only one in Pinner, so having cleared this hurdle with practically no effort at all I moved on to phase two.

This consisted of writing him a few lines to say how sorry I was to hear about the slipped disc, adding that in the circumstances we had decided to cancel the party. I did not specify what the circumstances were, judging it best to leave their precise definition to him, but continued as follows:

'Peter told me that you weren't so much ill as immobile and if he's right about that it's just possible that the time will soon begin to hang rather heavy and that you'd consider helping me out with a small personal problem for which you're certainly better qualified than anyone else I could ask. I won't bore you with the details now, but if later on you feel able to give me some professional advice do let me know. I should be more than grateful. Yours . . .'

I felt reasonably satisfied that he would rise to this bait, which I had purposely swathed in a certain amount of mystery, so as soon as the letter was posted I turned my attention to the next proposition, although, as it happened, I had barely got into my mental stride with it when there was a fresh development, requiring a fundamental change of strategy.

I was kneeling on the floor, altering the hem of a skirt, the kind of tedious job best not performed in Robin's presence lest he be driven into a dementia of nervous irritation, but which allows just the right amount of scope for the mind to range untrammelled, when he arrived home early from work and plopped the evening paper with deadly accuracy on the box of pins. Stifling the exclamations of rage and annoyance, I daintily moved it aside, but he said:

"No, go on, read it! There's something there to interest you."

"You mean the inquest? But I knew all about that in advance. Besides, I was there."

"Not the inquest, something new."

I spread out the paper and cast an eye over the front page. The banner headlines referred to a pile-up on a motorway, but further down and to the right of the page a more modest headline read as follows: 'Second Body Found in Thames'.

Beneath this were three short paragraphs, of which the first two had obviously been based on police handouts, stating merely that the body of John Masters, 23, of Warmenham-on-Thames, had been discovered by 56-year-old lock keeper, Mr Arthur Cook, in the early hours of Tuesday morning. He had been alerted to the tragedy by the sight of two wheels sticking up out of the water and investigation had confirmed that they were part of the invalid chair belonging to the deceased who, with his sister, Miss Chloe Masters, lived next door at Old Lock Cottage.

He and Miss Masters had between them managed to raise the wheel chair out of the river and had discovered the dead man strapped in the seat. Artificial respiration had proved futile. Asked whether he suspected foul play, Detective Superintendent Meiklejohn of the Thames Valley C.I.D. said it was too early to comment.

In his final paragraph the reporter drew the reader's notice to the startling coincidence of this discovery having been made only a few hours before the inquest on Michael Parsons, whose body had been recovered several miles upstream, the jury having subsequently returned a verdict of homicide. Asked about a possible connection between the two deaths, the police again refused to comment.

"You bet there's a connection," I said, dropping the paper and staring up at Robin, whose complacent expression showed that he was enjoying the sensation he had created quite as much as the expectation of dressmaking being abandoned for that evening. "The man who wrote this must be pretty dim. A child of ten could have found the connection with no help at all."

"I've no doubt you're right, but the libel laws being what they are the editor would need to be a child of ten to print it."

"Why? I mean, I can see that the personal angle might have been a bit risky, but there couldn't be anything libellous in revealing that one of the victims had worked for the same company as the sister of the other one."

"The company might not agree with you, nor the sister either. It would be rather suggestive."

"Of what?"

"General skulduggery around the film studio, for one thing. People might get the idea that she had pushed her brother overboard because he knew something which connected her with the other man's murder."

"But no one knew that the other one was a murder case when her brother died. It was only revealed hours later at the inquest."

"Really, Tessa, aren't you being the dim one now? The murderer didn't have to wait for the inquest to find out how Mike Parsons met his death. He or she would have known that perfectly well."

"So in that case why not have acted before? If her brother had really known something damning against her, I should have expected her to dispose of him ages ago. Why pick the very moment when, as you've pointed out, the two incidents couldn't fail to be connected?"

"Presumably because, if Chloe was responsible, she would have hoped that her brother's murder wouldn't be necessary. She could have gambled on Parsons never being found, or at any rate that so much time would have elapsed before he was that it would be impossible to establish the cause of death. The danger point for her would only have come when he was pulled out of the river within a week of his disappearance."

"Yes, I can understand all that, but what I still don't see is why her brother should only have become a danger to her then. If he knew she'd killed a man he might have blurted it out at any time, especially as he was given to hysterical tantrums."

"Oh, I don't suppose he would have known anything positive. It is more likely to have been some isolated piece of information, like her being away from the house during a certain period, which would have appeared quite innocent on its own, but would take on a more sinister aspect as soon as a dead man turned up."

"Well, you seem to have worked out a pretty firm case against Chloe. Is it still hypothetical, or do you know something that I don't?"

"No, I'm simply pointing out one of the conclusions which any logical mind could arrive at, once the link had been established between her and Mike Parsons."

"And what bothers me is that it is logical, and yet at the same time so absolutely false and incredible."

"That's more like it!"

"More like what?"

"Your true form. Finding something to be perfectly logical, and therefore to be instantly dismissed, is just what I have come to rely on."

"Because truth and logic are not necessarily synonymous."

"And your feminine intuition, or whatever name it goes by at this moment, tells you that Chloe was incapable of murdering her own brother?"

"No," I admitted slowly. "That's not so, now you mention it. I really believe she would be capable of murdering him for humane reasons; what they call a mercy killing in some circles. But I don't see her as a coward and I can't believe she would do such a thing simply to protect herself. Anyway, why couldn't it have been a straight-forward accident? The garden slopes straight down to the river and he might easily have lost control of his wheel chair and gone in by mistake."

"Except that people in their right minds, unless they happen to be professional escapists, don't strap themselves into a moving vehicle and then guide it full tilt towards a river."

"But Johnnie Masters wasn't in his right mind. From what Chloe told me, he was both subnormal and hysterical and, having had a brief glimpse of him, I can confirm it. He looked like a terrified zombie. If it wasn't an accident, I should say that suicide was the most likely explanation."

"There is a third possibility though, isn't there? Or rather a variation on your second. Namely, that he and his sister acted in collusion in murdering Parsons and when he knew the game was up he killed himself to avoid the consequences. How do you care for that?"

"Not bad. Chloe maintained that he still had the most tremendous crush on Mike, in spite of everything, but she could have been lying, I suppose. It was the one part of her story which couldn't be checked. I still think it would have been reckless of her to have been quite so frank in describing her motives for wanting Mike out of the way, but it's conceivable that she guessed they would come to light anyway and that she had nothing to lose by laying them all out herself. Not that I would repeat what she told me."

"One never knows what one may do until the circumstances arise," Robin reminded me. "But it might be interesting to know who else she has confided in."

"Certainly not Brenda."

"No, and that raises a question, doesn't it? Why not Brenda? She claims her relationship with Parsons was strictly platonic and yet, when he became such a menace, why didn't she appeal to his wife to control him? Wouldn't that have been the natural thing to do, if she had nothing to hide? Yet, as far as we know, she never made any attempt to get in touch with her."

"No one made any attempt to get in touch with her. She could as well have been the Man in the Iron Mask. And the single, universally known fact about her happens to have been a myth, although it was that which cut her off so effectively from the outside world."

"How do you know it was a myth?"

"Well, I don't really; at least, only in the negative sense that I've seen no evidence to support it. Tell me, though, Robin, how well informed are you on the subject of alcoholism?"

"About the same as most people. That's to say I know a good deal about the effects, a lot less about the causes."

"But even in your limited experience, would you have judged it possible for a long-standing addict to be able to drop it, just like that?"

"Not without fairly drastic treatment, no."

"You wouldn't for instance, imagine that a severe shock of some kind could have the same sobering up effect?"

"You mean like someone driving a car when he was drunk and running down a pedestrian?"

"Something like that."

"I suppose it's not unheard of. It might certainly contribute to a cure, but I still doubt if it would be a permanent one without medical treatment to back it up. Although that's precisely what you'd get, if you'd been responsible for an accident of that kind and been convicted of manslaughter. You'd get it over a long period in a prison hospital. On the other hand, if you're leading up to the proposition that Brenda killed her husband and pushed him in the river while under the influence and then, having realised her mistake, foreswore alcohol forever, I should forget it. I'm afraid anyone who was that drunk would have lacked the necessary co-ordination. Besides, I doubt if remorse, however intense, would have been enough. You'd need drugs and therapy on top of it to get you through. In fact, I suspect that in a case of that kind the true addict would very soon resort to the bottle in even larger quantities to try and obliterate the memory."

"Well, thank you," I said. "That's given me a few ideas to work on."

"So now you have completely resolved the Brenda paradox?"

"To tell you the truth, Robin, I felt I was making some headway with that already, but what you have just said has given me a new slant on Mike."

"Like who killed him, what for, and how, no doubt?"

"Yes, to one of your questions," I replied. "No, not yet to the other two, but I feel I'm making progress."

CHAPTER FOURTEEN

THE fish in the Pinner pool rose with a majestic leap within twenty-four hours of my casting the bait. There was some wriggling on the hook, however, for his proposal when he telephoned to thank me was that I should call at his home for a wee natter.

The prospect had only faint appeal, mainly because of fear of Madge being present in a chaperoning capacity, which would have an inhibiting effect on us both. So I insisted that I would not dream of invading his privacy, especially when he was unwell, and that my affairs could easily wait for a week or two. As an afterthought, I added that it would be impractical too, because there was a mass of claims and assessments which he would need to study and I should unfailingly leave the essential ones at home.

There was a brief lull in our conversation here and in the course of it Alec remembered that he had an appointment with his osteopath the following afternoon and, having remembered it, swam gracefully into the net by offering to call on me immediately afterwards. We settled for a dish of tea at Beacon Square between four and five o'clock and as soon as he had rung off I picked up the telephone again and dialled Brenda's number.

For the first time in my experience, she answered immediately, and then went straight into another string of complaints. It appeared that the Halifax contingent had left at dawn, to avoid the worst of the traffic, and that after only a few hours alone in the house she had already reached desperation point.

As usual, her plaintive, self-pitying tones jarred on the nerves and I heard myself saying:

"Now, come on, Brenda, take a pull. It can't be as bad as all that. After all, even when Mike was alive you were accustomed to spending long periods alone while the boys were at school."

"Yes, but that was different. I knew they'd be back at four and there was their tea to get, and usually Mike's supper to think about as well. I had things to keep me occupied, but now the hours just crawl. You don't know what it's like to be in this state."

This was unanswerable and I allowed her to go whining on, which she did by saying:

"Anyway, that was before we knew there was this murderer about. In those days I thought of murder as something that happened in the newspapers, but now I keep wondering all the time who he could be and who's next on the list."

"Do you mean you feel you might be in danger too?"

"Well, wouldn't you? If he's some kind of maniac who had a grudge against Mike, why stop there? That Superintendent Micki whatever his name is told me they were going to keep a watch on the house and I've seen one of their cars parked down by the corner of the field, but what's the good of that? What's to stop anyone creeping up here through the woods at the back, or even running me over when I go down to the shops? I bet you'd feel afraid if you were me."

Oddly enough, she was right, although I did not believe that her danger came from either of the two sources she had named, still less that there was anything I could do to avert it. However, I suggested driving down to keep her company for an hour or two, which she agreed to without much enthusiasm, and then I said:

"In the meantime, Brenda, perhaps it would be a good idea to give yourself a job of some kind."

"What? What are you talking about?"

"Well, I'm sure the house is already too spick and span to need any attention, but if you could find a few odds and ends to do in the garden it might take your mind off things."

I could almost feel her shudder and she said in a high-pitched voice,

"Oh no, not that, I couldn't possibly. It's worst of all in the garden. That hedge and everything . . . I sometimes think I'll never force myself to go near it again."

Conscious of having been a trifle insensitive, I endeavoured to make amends by leaving London with all speed, and arrived at Hill Grove exactly an hour and a half later.

The front door was locked and remained so until long after the last chime had died on the air, but the gloomy forebodings which this inspired were instantly wiped away by her appearance when she did arrive. She looked flustered, but had discarded her sunglasses for once and there was colour in her cheeks. Her hands were smudged and her hair dishevelled, making her look quite human, as well as a lot prettier than usual.

"I took your advice," she gabbled. "Set myself to a job of work. It wasn't a bad idea really, but I must look a sight. Mind waiting in the living room while I have a wash? Then I'll make some coffee."

"Oh, don't bother about that. Can't I give you a hand with whatever it is you're doing?"

"Well," she said doubtfully, "it would be nice to finish it, now I've got started. I don't know when I'll ever bring myself to go back to it. Fact is, I've been sorting out some of Mike's personal belongings. You know, clothes and that. The shoes are the worst problem. I don't believe they take them at the jumble, but I thought some of his other things might go. Come up and see what you think. Sooner or later I've got to make myself realise that I'm never going to see him again and I thought it might make it easier not having all these reminders of him everywhere I turn."

"Very wise. And if you're serious about giving some clothes away I do know a charity who would be delighted to get their hands on them."

"It seems wicked in a way, but I don't know of anyone who'd want to wear them and I don't suppose they'd fetch any cash. I suppose your place might be the best answer. The only trouble is getting them there. I don't much fancy carrying a lot of heavy parcels down to the post office on foot. Besides, it'll cost the earth in postal charges. Or do they pay those at the other end? They should do by rights, don't you think?"

"Perhaps so, but I'm afraid they don't. However, that's no worry because their headquarters are in Kensington, so if we pack them all into my car I can drop them off on my way home."

"Oh well, that's all right, then. Thanks."

"You'd better put some paper and string round them," I said, following her upstairs. "And make two separate parcels, while you're about it. Those which need cleaning in a separate one."

"Oh, they pay for the cleaning, do they? Well, that's something."

I did not disillusion her and she went on,

"Not that there'll be much needed in that way. Mike always saw to it himself. It was a habit he'd got into early on in life and he was fanatical about wearing anything that was the slightest bit soiled."

I cannot explain it but there are certain words in the English language which bring me out in a rash and soiled happens to be one of them. However, with a perversity which remains equally mysterious, the more her speech and attitudes jarred on me the greater my sense of obligation became. Perhaps it was because I could see nothing but wretchedness behind and ahead of her and other people's misfortunes always engender a sense of guilt.

"What's happened about your car?" I asked, when we had finished sorting the clothes and had carried the bundles downstairs.

"Still with the police. They take their time, don't they? Not that I want it here, I can tell you. Talk about bringing back memories! I just pray I never have to set eyes on it again. Besides, it's not as though it would be any use to me, as you know."

"Still, it might be a good idea to sell it and invest in a little second-hand one. You'd soon learn to drive, if you made up your mind to, and I should think you'd find it rather inconvenient living here without a car. But perhaps you haven't decided yet whether you will go on living here?"

"Whether I can afford to, you mean? No, but I've got to try and pull myself together and go into it properly in the next few days. I've got an appointment with the bank manager tomorrow. He rang me just after you did. Wants to talk to me about the will. It seems Mike made him executor, or whatever they call it."

"Well, that's lucky because he'll know better than anyone how to advise you."

"Think so? Well, maybe. I daresay Mike wouldn't have done it if he hadn't thought it was for the best. Now, the other thing that's bothering me, Tessa, is what to do about these books."

We had moved into the living room by this time and the reference was to half a dozen hard-backed volumes, with about twice the number of paperbacks, which were stacked on the floor by the bookcase.

"You surely don't intend to turn those out as well? Why not keep them for the boys when they're old enough?"

"Because they aren't mine to keep. These are some that Mike borrowed from the American chap . . . Drew Somebody . . . lives up the road."

"Well, I don't suppose he's in any hurry for them."

"No, but that's not the point," Brenda said obstinately. "I don't like the idea of other people's possessions lying around."

"Okay, so why not shove them in a carrier and take them back?"

"I could do, I suppose, but I'd be sure to run into her and I'd feel so awkward."

"For heaven's sake, why?"

"She might think it was just an excuse to worm my way in. They never had any time for me when Mike was alive and I don't want their pity now. I'd rather things stayed as they are. To tell you the truth, I wondered if you'd mind dropping them off for me? It's number 19, about half way up, and you can recognise the place a mile off by all the old junk they leave lying around in the front garden. You wouldn't need to go indoors, just dump the books on the doorstep. They'll know where they came from and it couldn't make the place look more untidy than it does already."

I did not tell her so, but in fact I had no intention of leaving them on the doorstep, and moreover was hoping to find both the Burnetts at home when I carried out my errand. It was partly for this reason that I did not go straight to their house after leaving Brenda. Another was that it was getting on for five o'clock and I realised that all the cleaners' shops would be closed by the time I reached London. I did not much relish the idea of storing Mike's clothes at Beacon Square overnight, still less of Robin's finding them on the back seat, if he should decide to use the car. Fortunately, there was a simple way out of the dilemma and having driven half way up the hill and past number 19, I reversed into an open driveway and drove smartly down again, turning left into the main road and the new shopping centre.

It covered quite a small area, about half way between a village and a minor suburb and all the buildings were brand new and of crushing mediocrity, but it was not only this which depressed me. Even worse was the feeling it gave me of belonging to another age, for I found myself contrasting it with the kind of High Street conglomeration which would have served a community of this size in my childhood. Then there would have been lots of small shops, each selling a separate type of commodity, all dotted about in a haphazard fashion and interspersed with private houses and cottages. Here the whole area was given over to commerce, with one large and one small supermarket cheek by jowl, and two other chain stores opposite them. There were also numerous banks, a travel bureau and driving school, and a car park flanked on one side by red brick public lavatories.

There was a choice of two dry cleaners, Streamline and Quickservice. The girl behind the counter of the first one did not do much for the image, for she was fat and pasty faced, bulging out of her tight trousers and grubby, sleeveless white satin blouse. She was also extremely sluggish and deliberate in her movements, raising up each separate garment in slow motion and carefully inspecting it for indelible stains and breakable buttons, before thumbing through a three-page price list and writing out the ticket.

It was therefore all the more gratifying when this boring performance ended on a somewhat sensational note. She had worked her way through to the last item to be cleaned, which happened to be a blue and red striped dressing gown and was in the act of lifting it up by the shoulder seams when her expression slowly but perceptibly changed. She then dropped the dressing gown back on the counter as though it had burned her fingers. "You did say the name was Price?"

Since I had already repeated it four times, there was little point in denying it now and I nodded.

"Funny! Looks just the same."

"Same as what?"

"One we had in for cleaning only the week before last. Customer was in a hurry and wanted it done express, I remember. It looked just like this one. Same label too."

"Oh well," I explained hastily, "that's possible. I've brought these for a friend, you see. She's without a car at the moment and I said I'd drop them off for her."

"I should think she might have made a mistake with this one. Probably doesn't realise he'd brought it in himself. Think you ought to take it back?"

"No time, I'm afraid. Just throw it in with the rest, if you don't mind."

"Okay," she replied indifferently and went laboriously through the business of copying the details on to her pad, then tore out each individual receipt and handed them over.

"Ready Thursday, but it's early closing and we shut at one."

"Right," I said, already half way to the door, but it was not quite over yet.

"Just a sec.," she called out. "What about this, then?"

I turned to see her holding out a small folded square of blue paper.

"Better take it, hadn't you? Might be something important?"

"Yes, it might. Where did you find it?"

"In one of the pockets."

"You're quite the most thorough person I ever met," I assured her. "Wasted in a place like this."

I did not unfold the paper until I was back in the car, but trotted along, laying bets with myself as to what it would contain. Winning them too, as it turned out, for the inside of the paper was covered with half a dozen lines of flamboyant, instantly recognisable script, filling the top half of a torn off sheet of writing paper. The message began and ended in the middle of sentences, but it was of no consequence, for I could make a fair guess at the beginning of the first one, having already seen the end of the last. The part of the letter now in my hands read as follows:

'. . . true that he still has the greatest affection for you, but it can only end in more disillusionment for him, and personally I consider that he has a better chance of recovery if you will consent to leave him alone. To be as blunt as I know how, I am asking one last favour of you—that you will stay away from us, just as I mean never to speak to you again for . . .'

The only small puzzle was how this fragment came to be in the pocket of a dressing gown which had been returned from the cleaners only such a short time before Mike's death. However, I shelved that problem for the time being, for there was reading matter of a different nature to be undertaken before I paid my next call.

CHAPTER FIFTEEN

SUCH bonuses do not fall into one's lap every time, however, and I soon discovered that by timing my call on the Burnetts for half past five I had missed my chance of coming face to face with the elusive sergeant by only a few minutes. Fay, who opened the door to me, with Claire balanced on her left hip, explained that he had been home all afternoon, but that this was the one day of the week he had to work nights.

She was very cordial though and, having thanked me profusely for returning the books, bade me come along in and meet the rest of the brood. She then led the way to the kitchen, a brief journey which nevertheless provided enough contrasts with the Parsons' menage to satisfy the most avid student of human nature.

In addition to the baby's push chair, there were two dolls' prams lined up in the hall, plus a selection of mangled toys and picture books scattered over the floor and staircase. At the foot of the stairs a pugnacious look-ing dog on wheels barred the way with a ferocious glassy stare and there was ample evidence in the way of rubber bones and muddy paw prints to show that the household also included at least one dog which was not on wheels.

Two whey-faced, wispy little girls, introduced to me as Louise and Mary Jane, were seated at the kitchen table. Both had flaxen hair like Claire's and black circles under their eyes and in general there appeared to have been a skimping of flesh and blood all round, giving rise to the idea that there was not quite enough to go round among three of them, but that by putting the mixture together and starting again, one respectably plump and sturdy infant might emerge.

I accepted a glass of milk, which appeared to be the popular beverage and Fay requested Louise and Mary Jane to take their beakers and peanut butter sandwiches and run along and watch T.V. for a while. She then deposited Claire in a circular contraption which looked rather like a giant butterfly net and invited me to fill her in with the current situation chez Parsons. After I had done so she said:

"Well, she sounds to be making out better than I'd have imagined. From the way Mike always hinted . . ."

"That she was a drunk?"

"Right. That is, he never said so to me, as I recall, but Drew certainly had that impression. It was mainly why he got to feel so sorry for him."

"Did he feel sorry for him?"

"Oh, sure! I mean, he was grateful to him at the start. He thought it was darn nice and neighbourly of him to keep dropping around and taking him down to the pub and all, but there were times, you know how it is, when he didn't feel like going out of an evening. Often he'd have preferred to stay home with me and the girls, only he didn't care to hurt Mike's feelings. Finally, I'd say it was Mike who got to be so dependent on Drew, instead of the other way round."

"Which pub did they frequent, do you know?"

"Different ones, I guess, but there was one special place Drew told me about. A real old-fashioned country inn down by the river with everyone drinking beer and joining in the darts game."

"That's another thing I meant to ask you; what did they drink on these outings?"

"Oh, Drew always had beer. He's hooked on your English beer now, even likes it warm. Just wait till the folks back home get to hear about that!" she said, smiling at her own joke.

"And Mike too?"

"No, he stuck to ginger ale, that kind of thing. Drew used to tease him about it at first, but then he discovered that Mike had gone teetotal to try and help his wife. He admired him for that. Me too, but all the same . . ."

"What?"

"Well, you know how it is? I ought not to be saying this now he's dead, and he certainly did have problems, but have you ever noticed how some people can get so involved in their own problems that they end by acting as though it gave them special rights and privileges?"

"Yes, I had noticed it."

"Sometimes I thought that applied to Mike. Like I said, there were plenty of evenings when Drew would really rather have stayed home and cut out the pub crawl, but he always gave in finally. It wasn't only because he liked Mike and felt sorry for him. There was this other aspect where Mike made you feel you had an obligation to do whatever he wanted. I feel wicked saying this, I honestly do, but I won't be entirely sorry not to have him turning up on the doorstep two or three times a week."

CHAPTER SIXTEEN

"ALTHOUGH I suppose one must assume that people don't go about killing their neighbours just for the sake of a few quiet domestic evenings," I remarked later that evening. "Even though Drew is such a promising name, and even though he is a man."

"I am not sure that I care very much for that last observation," Robin said. "Admittedly, most murders are committed by men, but it doesn't follow that most men are potential murderers."

"Oh, I know that. At least, I think I do, but it has always seemed to me that in this case in particular so much sheer physical strength would have been needed, much more than the average woman possesses. Even suffocating a fairly young and able-bodied man would surely require a good deal of force, quite apart from carting the corpse around afterwards and finally hoisting it into the river? In that way the evidence does rather point to a man, although not necessarily this one."

"So having straightened out that small point, why do you say that Drew is such a promising name?"

"Simply because he's the only person I've come across so far who could very easily be masquerading as this mysterious Sandy. The one, according to Brenda, whose first call came through a telephone switchboard and who has a slight American accent. I should explain that I had a careful look through all those books which Brenda asked me to return and one of them had an interesting inscription on the flyleaf."

"Are there no limits to your inquisitiveness?"

"Absolutely not, and I don't imagine there are to yours when you're tracking down the miscreants. Except that you would probably call it fact finding."

"And what facts did you uncover this time?" Robin asked, proving my point.

"Oh, plenty. One was that his birthday is on 12th December, another that he had an aunt called Helen, who was sufficiently attached to him four years ago to mark the occasion with a book on water fowl, costing fifteen dollars. The really stunning one was that to this Aunt Helen he is known as Andrew. 'Happy birthday to Andrew' is what she wrote, 'With love from Aunt Helen', and the date underneath."

"Quite a little potted biography! Which is the relevant bit?"

"In the name. You see, when Brenda mentioned this Sandy with the American accent I immediately began to wonder about those neighbours Mike had become so chummy with, although at the time I couldn't see any reason why the man should call himself Sandy. Drew, all by itself, is not such an uncommon name in America, as you probably know, and it didn't occur to me that he might actually have started life as Andrew."

"And when it did you instantly concluded that another nickname might be Sandy?"

"Not exactly, but I do think it's possible that Brenda could have heard it in that way. If somebody said to you on the telephone 'This is Andy', you can see how easily the last two words would run together."

"Yes, I suppose so, but why should Mike Parsons have called him Andy when to everyone else he was Drew?"

"There's no proof of that. All we know for certain is that his wife refers to him as Drew, and that might be her own special name for him. On the other hand, from what I'm beginning to learn about Mike it wouldn't surprise me if he was another one who used special names for his close friends. He seems to have had a passion for insinuating himself into other people's lives and this could have been one of the devices he used to make his relationship with them exclusive."

"Why didn't you settle the matter by putting a few tactful questions to Mrs Burnett?"

"Because the idea only came to me when I was half way home. Never mind, I'll probably drum up an excuse to go and call on her again. Although I do hope I shall be proved wrong."

"A forlorn hope, no doubt! What inspires it?"

"Just that I like Fay. She's got twenty times more guts than that self-pitying old Brenda and it would be awful if it turned out that her husband was involved in a murder."

"It doesn't follow. There's nothing incriminating in ringing someone up and saying your name is Andy, and as you've pointed out the only motive you've been able to hang on him so far is decidedly thin."

"I know, but if it was him the fact that he telephoned Brenda within hours of Mike's disappearance and again on the day he turned up in the river does look rather fishy. You could almost believe that he'd got the wind up and was trying to find out through Brenda whether there'd been any developments. However, at least there can't be any connection between him and Chloe's brother, so that's one point in his favour."

"Only half a point, really. The odds now stand at a thousand to one against the two deaths being linked."

"Since when?"

"Since the experts went to work on the suicide note. They're satisfied that it's genuine and furthermore the G.P. has gone on record as stating that the boy was in a highly neurotic condition, with pronounced suicidal tendencies."

"But Robin, darling, this is the first I've heard of any note. Why didn't you tell me?"

"Mainly because I knew you would say it was a forgery."

"And why do you think I won't say it now?"

"Because now you would be voicing the opinion of an amateur, who has not seen it, in direct contradiction to all the handwriting experts who have."

"Oh, all right, but what did it say?"

"Just what you'd expect. All the usual stuff about being a burden to himself and everyone else. You know how it goes?"

"No mention of Mike?"

"Not as far as I know. I'm another one who hasn't seen it, but I understand no one was specifically named. It was addressed to the coroner, incidentally, and the only point which need concern us is that its authenticity has been proved beyond doubt."

"I wonder they can be so sure. They can't have had many samples to compare it with."

"That's where you're so wrong. It's true there wasn't all that much to go on, but he used to write occasional notes and postcards to his sister from the home he was in before the operation. They were mainly to ask her to bring something special next time she went to visit him, quite trivial things like that, but apparently she'd kept a few of them."

"I wonder why?"

"Well, not everyone is methodical about destroying old letters. But I can tell how your mind is working and I must break it to you that the comparison didn't rest solely on the samples which Chloe was able to produce. The invalid home came up with some specimens too. One of their therapy exercises was to get the patients to write little essays about their favourite television programmes and so forth. They found an exercise book with quite a collection of them written by Masters."

"I see. So you think we should put that whole episode down to coincidence? I mean, the manner of his death and the timing of it, plus the very special relationship between him and Mike?"

"No, that would be a bit too much to swallow, wouldn't it? I think there probably was a link, in so far as Parsons' fading out of the boy's life at such a tricky time was all he needed to screw himself up to commit suicide. And the ironic thing is, you know, Tessa, that he could have been unaware that Parsons was even officially missing. When he ceased to come around any more Chloe might well have worked on her brother to accept the fact gradually, before she broke the news to him. Don't you think that's possible?"

"Maybe," I admitted. "But I don't know why, something you said perhaps, tells me the answer is not quite as simple as that. I can't put my finger on it, but I feel it in my bones."

"Oh, why not give your poor old bones a rest for once? Let's forget about murders and suicides for a bit and go out on the town. Where would you like to have dinner?"

I agreed that he had the right idea. It was high time to get out of the rut, and furthermore there is no surer way of finding the answer to a puzzle than by ceasing to think about it, which is exactly what happened in this case.

CHAPTER SEVENTEEN

ALEC arrived the next day on the stroke of four-thirty. I was ready and waiting for him, with a tea tray on one end of the dining room table and a pile of income tax documents on the other, but once the preparatory stages were over, nothing went according to plain.

This was only partly due to the fact that his bearing did not suggest that of a man with a slipped disc. He looked a little strained and careworn, but his back was straight and his movements relatively fluid. However, when I congratulated him on this he reacted very irritably and brushed my remarks aside as though they had been made expressly to taunt him. I concluded from this that the pretence of illness was so thin that even casual acquaintances were not expected to be deceived by it, and I therefore invited him to sit down and take a preliminary look through my papers while I made a pot of tea.

I had not worked out a formula for introducing the topic of Mike's death, believing that it was bound to arise naturally in the course of things and that it was preferable that he should be the one to bring it up. The assumption had been that when I returned with the tea he would ask me one or two more or less pertinent questions about my financial affairs, would pick out a selection of documents to take home for further study and that after making some assessment of the amount of work required of him we should glide politely through the matter of his fee and settle down to a cosy chat over the teacups.

However, on my return, after a somewhat longer interval than I had anticipated owing to Mrs Cheeseman's having hit on an entirely new hiding place for the sugar, I found him staring moodily into space and paying not the smallest attention to the task I had set him.

After an uncomfortable silence he said harshly,

"And now perhaps you would be good enough to tell me what this is all about?"

"But I have told you, Alec. My tax situation has got into a proper mess and I was hoping you could help me to sort it out."

"There's no mess that I can see."

"That's because you haven't given yourself enough time. You can't have been through that lot already?"

"No, maybe not, but I can see from the correspondence that you already have a firm of accountants handling your affairs, and very reputable people they are too."

"A bit too reputable, in my opinion. They're so stuffy that I sometimes wonder whose side they're on."

"Well, in my opinion, you'll not improve your position by taking your business elsewhere."

"That wasn't exactly my intention. All I really want is to jerk them up a bit. You see, the situation has changed now that Robin and I are taxed separately. I have to put in all my own expense claims and so on and I don't think they're making them nearly stiff enough. They take the attitude that actors have such a lovely time prancing about and doing their own thing that they're lucky to get paid at all, and the trouble is that I don't know enough about the law to point out where they've slipped up. That's how I thought you might be able to help. After all, you know the form about our profession, if anyone does."

"Then I must inform you that you were very gravely mistaken. If you're looking for someone to conspire with you in tax evasion you've come to the wrong party."

"Oh goodness, Alec, don't say such terrible things. There's no question of tax evasion, I just feel that I am being asked to pay more than I legally need to. I could be wrong, of course, but in that case I'd at least like the satisfaction of having it properly explained to me by someone who knows the score. That's really all."

"If you want my advice, there's no but one way to get it. It'll mean your sitting down now to write to your accountants informing them that you no longer require their services. And you follow it up with a letter to the Inspector of Taxes, notifying him that I am empowered to act on your behalf. Is that what you want?"

"No, I hadn't envisaged anything quite so drastic as that. It's not the kind of step I could take without consulting Robin," I said, falling back on a well worn path of retreat. "All I really wanted from you was a few tips, more or less as between friends."

"And you consider me your friend?"

"Shouldn't I?"

"If that's friendship, give me enemies. I was prepared to let you have the benefit of the doubt, but now I'm here I'm bound to say I consider this to be nothing but a lot of trumped up nonsense."

"Okay, Alec, so I made a stupid gaffe and I'm sorry, but there's no need to go on like that."

"No one likes to be taken for a fool."

"But I don't do anything of the kind. Would I have asked for your help, if I had? It's I who am the fool for misunderstanding the situation, but that was sheer ignorance, not malice. Now that you've made your position clear, can't we just drop the subject and talk about something else?"

"No, I'll be on my way now, if you've no objection."

"Oh, but I have every objection. You must at least have a cup of tea before you go, to show there's no ill feeling."

He had jerked himself upright, but now subsided again, accepting the cup which I held out to him and saying softly:

"You may rest assured that my staying will not be for that reason."

"Oh God, don't tell me you're still furious? I told you it was a mistake and that I apologise."

"Not furious, no; curious would be the better word. I'm wondering what your game is. I said I didn't care to be taken for a fool and I don't take you for one either. I'd awfully like to know what all this was in aid of. Did your husband put you up to it?"

"Good heavens, no, I haven't even discussed it with him. I expect I would have mentioned it, if you had agreed to help me, but there'll be no point in doing so now, will there?"

"I'm not referring to your income tax. Let's forget about that despicable little pretence now, shall we?"

"Oh, by all means, if you're determined to be offensive; but in that case what were you referring to?"

"Your motive in tricking me into coming here. You told me your husband was a policeman, I believe. Did he by any chance instruct you to set a trap for me, so that I might inadvertently betray something?"

I was so thoroughly taken aback by this accusation, and yet at the same time so eager to find out whether an imaginary trap could have the same result as a genuine one that I did not dare meet his eye for fear of betraying something on my own side and hastily covered up by pouring out a second cup of tea, while saying:

"I'm sorry, Alec, but I've completely lost the thread. What can you be talking about?"

"That hasn't answered my question."

"Oh, very well, will this do? I swear on my oath that I have not mentioned one word about you to Robin. He hardly knows of your existence and he has no idea that you are here. That's a promise and I just hope it makes you feel better."

No assurances to this effect were forthcoming, however, and when I looked up, I saw that his expression was both hostile and wary. Still in the same quiet and threatening tone, he said:

"And from the wee insight you were considerate enough to give me into your financial standing, it's plain that you're not short of money, so presumably we can discount blackmail. What does that leave, I wonder?"

This time I was so utterly dumbfounded that I literally could not think of any reply and before I could pull myself together the silence was shattered by the slam of the front door.

It caused my heart to give the most sickening leap and it did not regain its normal position among the rest of the organs after I had risked a glance at Alec. There was really no reason why Robin should not return to his own house at any time he chose, with or without warning me in advance, but in fact he very rarely did so at five o'clock in the afternoon and, no question about it, this was a most unfortunate day to have made the exception. Alec was half out of his chair again, moving with a speed which indicated definitively that all discs were in place, and his complexion had turned the colour of concrete. The anger and dislike were no longer visible in his expression. Doubtless they were still there in full measure, but the emotion which topped all else was fear.

"Well," I squeaked. "Well, what do you know? What an extraordinary . . ."

At which point the door opened and in marched Toby.

His eyes bulged slightly as he took in the tableau, and practically started out of his head as Alec sank back into his chair and buried his face in his hands, while I reeled backwards in a fair imitation of Lady Macbeth catching sight of the dagger.

Unaccustomed to his entrances creating such a sensational effect, Toby said coldly:

"I am sorry if I startled you, but I thought it would save trouble if I used my key. Not so, apparently. Would you prefer me to go out and come in again, or go out and stay out?"

"Neither," I fluttered. "It's perfectly all right, nothing wrong at all. You gave us rather a fright, you see. We thought you were Robin. My husband, you know."

"Yes, indeed, I had heard."

"And I'd just been saying that I wasn't expecting him for hours."

"Oh well, that explains everything, I suppose."

Whether it did or not was a matter of stark indifference to me, but I was relieved to see that it had had a reviving effect on the one for whom it was designed. Alec slowly lifted his head and stared at me briefly, before turning to look at Toby, as I went burbling on:

"I don't believe you've met Alec Ferguson, have you? This is my cousin, Toby Crichton, Alec. He writes plays, in case you're interested."

"I hardly see why he should be," Toby remarked.

"You never know. Some people take a great interest in how other people earn their living."

"Oh that, yes; but I don't see what it has to do with writing plays."

"Never mind, the tide may turn in your favour one day, and in the meantime it's a profession, isn't it? Just as much as being an actor or a policeman, and that's what counts."

"Oh, is it?" he asked, still looking extremely puzzled, not apparently having caught on to the fact that the purpose of all this badinage was to get it through to Alec that he had not been tricked, and thus enable him to get a grip on himself. That it was partially successful was seen a moment later when he stood up, looking shaky still and a bit hunted, but able to conduct himself with reasonable composure.

"Well, I think that about finishes our business," he told me, making a brave attempt to sound casual. "There'll be no necessity for me to call again. Good day to you both."

"I'll see you out," I said, following him into the hall, but Toby had left the chain off and Alec wrenched the front door open and having passed through it hurtled down the steps to the pavement without a backward glance.

When he was out of sight I closed the door again and returned to the dining room with a slow and thoughtful gait.

"Who was that? Some criminal on the run, I take it?" Toby enquired, having evidently done some thinking on his own behalf.

"Yes," I replied, "I imagine so."

"Not very attractive manners. I wonder you bother to harbour him?"

"I wasn't harbouring him exactly."

"Nevertheless, you were at great pains to convince him that I was not a member of the constabulary."

"Yes, I know. I should have remembered that he has a positive phobia about them, and I do wish I knew why. But I acted in self-interest, really. I didn't fancy the idea of his losing his head and trying to shoot his way out."

"No, we shouldn't have liked that at all. Has he really sunk so low? Perhaps it's just as well I arrived in the nick of time?"

"I can't agree; and what are you doing here, anyway?"

"I was hungry. I thought we might go to some smart restaurant this evening, if Robin's free. Why can't you agree?"

"Because if you hadn't stepped in when you did I might have uncovered something. I feel I was on the brink of breaking through his defences."

"I am not sure that's the sort of brink to do you much good. Why not just hand him over to Robin?"

"Perhaps I will in the end, but there's a little matter I want to settle first, as soon as possible in fact. Are you staying the night?"

"Yes, if you've no objection."

"Then don't let me keep you. You must be eager to unpack and put on a clean shirt. I think you will find everything in order in the spare room."

As soon as he had gone I sprang to the telephone and dialled the number of my old friend, Gerald Pettigrew. Not only is he my old friend, but he is also a very shrewd and sought after lawyer.

"Have you time to listen to a short story, Gerald? It won't take more than five minutes."

"So long as it hasn't an X certificate, carry on, old top."

When I had outlined the facts, I asked: "So if I had called his bluff and appointed him my official accountant, would he have been entitled to act for me?"

"How would I know, old lady?"

"Well, really, Gerald, I thought that's what solicitors were for. I mean, it does have some bearing on the law, doesn't it?"

"Yes, yes, yes, but you haven't given me nearly enough gen. If the chap's a qualified and registered chartered accountant, then the answer is yes. If not, not. That's the long and short of it."

"Well, could you find out whether he's in the long or the short category?"

"Might do. What's in it for me?"

"Only my undying love and gratitude."

"Blimey! I don't half have to work hard for them! Go ahead, then. Give me the full name, approximate age and any other details that spring to mind and I'll get him looked up for you."

"You're an angel, Gerald."

CHAPTER EIGHTEEN

THERE was no word from Brenda on Friday and since that day marked the start of one of Robin's rare long weekends off duty, we went down to Sussex to spend it with an elderly and dotty relative, not returning to Beacon Square until late on Monday night.

Soon after nine the next morning I tried to telephone her, but there was no reply, which made me a trifle uneasy and this, combined with the fact that I still had a parcel to collect from Streamline, dictated the next move. Delaying only to get the salt washed out of my hair and to lunch with my agent, who had no words of comfort for me and did not even offer to pay her share of the bill, I set forth once again in the direction of Hill Grove.

It was after four by the time I arrived at the cleaners, and obviously a peak period in the new shopping centre. The pavements were thronged with young women pushing loaded prams, or dragging older children by the hand, and with middle-aged women hoisting along a dog, or a basket on wheels, in their wake.

When I had negotiated my way through this chaotic scene up to the doors of Streamline I was disgusted to find at least four customers ahead of me. Most of them looked as though they had been there for hours and Miss Pasty Face was right on form, traipsing lethargically away to the back premises and remaining concealed there for long periods while she tracked down each individual garment, before returning to the counter to strip it of its tags, cellophane cover and wire coat hanger.

When it finally came to my turn the red and blue striped dressing gown was the first article to be retrieved and after she had sauntered away again, I picked it up and slung it over my arm, hoping at least to save the two minutes required for parcelling it up. I then returned to my position by the window, cursing the whim which had brought me to this establishment rather than its rival across the road.

The strange thing was that only a moment later I had cause to reverse this verdict, for had I then been standing in the premises of Messrs. Quickservice I should certainly not have seen a familiar figure emerge from a building a few doors down from it. She was holding a manila envelope which she thrust into her bag, as she turned and walked away towards the car park.

A quick look at the counter revealed that Miss Streamline had not returned and I scuttled out of the shop and had pushed my way through half a dozen separate groups before realising that I was still holding the dressing gown. There was nothing to be done about it, however, because, as is so often the case, one side of the road was much more favoured by the pram and poodle brigade than the other, and in this respect my quarry had the advantage of me. Only the fact that she was unaware of being pursued and so had no reason to hurry and that I, having guessed her destination, could concentrate exclusively on darting in and out of the human traffic enabled me to catch up with her. Furthermore, I had retained a clear visual memory of the car she would be making for and in fact she was actually unlocking the driver's door when I rounded the corner of the public lavatories and then abruptly switched to a normal walking pace.

"Oh, hallo!" I said, strolling up to her in a leisurely fashion.

She was behind the wheel by this time, but had not yet closed the door and I grasped the handle in an absent minded way and pulled it a little further open.

There was an agonised silence and then she said:

"Oh, hallo, Tessa! What are you doing in these parts?"

"Visiting Mike's widow. I think she's in a poor way. You know, too sunk in misery even to go out and buy food. I've stopped off here to gather up a few supplies."

"Oh, I see. Well, rather you than me," Chloe said, making a gesture towards closing the door.

Hanging on to it with might and main, I said: "I was just leaving when I saw you getting into your car, so I took the opportunity to come over and say how sorry I was to hear about your brother."

"Thanks."

"I ought to have written really, but it's so difficult to know what to say to people."

"That's all right. I didn't expect a letter."

"All the same, I truly am sorry. It must have been a hideous shock for you."

"Yes, it was, but I'm getting over it now. As you know, he wasn't a normal young man. It would be hypocrisy to pretend that he had very much to live for. It's a help to know that in many ways he's much better off where he is."

"Why, yes, I suppose that is the most sensible way of looking at it. And what now? Are you planning to go abroad?"

She had made another tentative move to shut the door, but the force suddenly went out of it and she dropped her hand back on the wheel, saying sharply:

"No. What gave you that idea?"

"Oh, simply that I thought I saw you coming out of the travel bureau just now. I thought you might be planning a trip somewhere, to get right away from things for a bit."

"Then you guessed wrong. It's the last thing I have in mind. Apart from anything else, I couldn't afford it and the first priority is to get back to work. You must have mistaken me for someone else."

She was wearing a white dress with a green chiffon scarf in the neck and green shoes, so it was not very likely that I could have, but I did not exasperate her further by persisting. I considered that she would have quite enough exasperation to contend with on the journey home, when she flayed herself for denying the charge quite so vehemently and in quite such detail. So I allowed her to tug the door shut at last and to slam the car into gear.

There was of course nothing to prevent my going back to the travel agents to verify the matter for myself, but it hardly seemed worth the bother, since even an affirmative would still have left the burning question unanswered. At that moment I would have parted with all my worldly goods to know why Chloe had looked so utterly stricken when I had first accosted her.

CHAPTER NINETEEN

THERE was a film of dust on the birchwood coffee table, the fan of pleated paper covering the fireplace was more grey than white and the pile of magazines slightly out of alignment. It would have been logical to assume that Brenda was now so dispirited as to have gone beyond the healing powers of dusting and scrubbing, but this was not the case. On the contrary, the housekeeping obsession seemed to have diminished as her hopes rose and I found her, if far from cheerful, in a more calm and resolute mood than at any previous time. I explained that I had been worried by not getting any reply to my telephone call and she said:

"Oh, I expect I was down seeing the bank manager. Didn't I tell you I had an appointment with him?"

"Yes, you did, but I thought that was last week."

"So it was, but I had to go back for another interview this morning. So many papers to sign, you wouldn't believe! I thought my hand would drop off."

"I hope it all adds up to good news?"

"Well, not quite so bad as I'd expected, let's say. None of it takes the place of having Mike back, but I will admit it's a relief to know we shan't be thrown out on the streets. There's a bit more in his deposit account than he'd let on and A.I.P. have been awfully good. I had a letter from them this morning saying they were going to pay me six months of his salary in a lump sum. Wonders will never cease!"

"I'm so glad. And that probably means that you won't have to worry about looking for a job, at least not immediately."

"Oh yes, I will. Don't run away with the idea that I'm going to be comfortably off or anything like that. It'll be an awful struggle, specially with the boys getting big and needing so many clothes and everything. But the bank says that what I ought to do is use this windfall from the company to pay off most of the mortgage, and then I might just be able to manage on what I can earn, with the interest from the capital."

"Well, that's marvellous. There must be quite a hefty sum?"

"Like I say, a bit more than I'd expected. Mike never breathed a word, but it seems he's been depositing quite large sums in cash over the last year or so. The manager couldn't account for it, except he thought it might be that Mike had lent somebody some money a long time ago and these were the repayments. Long time ago is right, for I can't see Mike being able to dole out sums like that once we'd got married and bought this house. I bet whoever it is won't keep up the repayments now, though. Still, mustn't grumble, must I? We shan't have to lose our home and that's the main thing."

"Yes, indeed. I couldn't be more delighted."

"I'll be able to pay back your loan, of course," Brenda said stiffly, as though this might have been the thought behind my rejoicing.

"Oh, forget it, there's no hurry whatever. It's simply that I'm pleased for your sake. As you say, none of it will bring him back, but it's great to know that some things will go on just the same and that you'll have a certain amount of security."

"Oh yes, but for how long I don't know, with prices shooting up the way they are! Still, I've been thinking over what you said about buying a car. I always take your advice, don't I? Perhaps I'll ask my brother-in-law to look out for some cheap little second-hand one. It might be a saving in the end, with fares going up too."

"Very good idea. You won't get nearly so depressed and lonely when you're mobile, and it will make all the difference to the boys."

"Well, I wouldn't bother if it wasn't for them, would I? The trouble is, I don't know whether I'll ever master the driving well enough to pass the test; and another worry is how I'm going to afford driving lessons. I went into the motoring school after I left the bank this morning and they told me it takes at least twelve lessons for the average person of my age. Sometimes as many as fifteen. I daresay I'll need even more than that, being such a nit about mechanical things. Mike did his best to teach me several times, but it was hopeless."

"Well, that's often the case between husbands and wives, but it's a pity you haven't got some friend who would let you practise on their car. That's really the only way to cut down on lessons."

"Well, I haven't. Not a single one that I'd care to ask such a favour of. And I can't see my sister letting me near their precious car when I go up to stay with them. No, I can't think of anyone."

"Well, I can," I said. "How about me?"

"You? Oh no, I couldn't possibly, Tessa."

"Why not? In fact, what's to stop us having a go now, this minute?"

"Oh no, I wouldn't dare, honestly. Besides, isn't it against the law to drive without those L plates?"

"Not so long as we keep off the road. We can see about those later on, when you've got the hang of it. Just for today you can practise starting and stopping in the drive."

"What about your car though? I'd be scared stiff of smashing it up. Suppose I forgot which one was the brake and couldn't stop?"

"Never fear, I'll be ready with the handbrake. And you're much more likely to stall the engine and stop of your own accord. That's what beginners usually do."

CHAPTER TWENTY

"AND beginner she most definitely was," I reported to Robin. "So there's another possibility gone up in smoke!"

"What possibility is that?"

"The one I mistakenly got hold of when you were reading out the list of things they found in Mike's car. If you remember, it included the Highway Code, which struck me as odd at the time because it's more a thing you'd associate with a learner driver than a fully fledged one and it occurred to me that Brenda might have been lying when she said she couldn't drive and had secretly been taking lessons. Starting with that, I worked it out that she could conceivably have driven their own car down to the Strand with Mike's body dumped in the back."

"I suppose you'd gone a bit further with it than that?"

"Oh yes, a lot. Let's suppose, for the sake of argument, that she'd returned to the house after seeing the boys off to school and found him still asleep in bed, perhaps snoring with his mouth open, or something equally disagreeable, and a sort of madness had come over her, so that she'd seized the pillow and held it down over his face until he'd stopped breathing. Then afterwards she'd have been faced with the problem of disposing of him, and so I thought she might just have left him covered up in the bed and told Barry and Keith that he'd gone to work after all. The garage would have been locked anyway, so they couldn't have known the car was still inside. Then around midnight, when all the houses in sight had their lights off, she might have hauled him downstairs to the garage."

"Wouldn't that have woken the children? She's no amazon, by the sound of it, and dragging a dead body down a flight of stairs would have involved a fair amount of thumping and bumping."

"Well, I don't know, Robin. Perhaps she could have thrown him out of the window?"

"But even though he was dead, I think the effects of a fall like that would have shown up in the p.m., you know. Also there would still have been the business of dragging him to the car, and out again and into the river when she arrived there. No mean feat for a single-handed female, but I suppose your answer to that would be that she used the missing punt pole to push him off the bank and into the flowing part of the river?"

"No, as it happens, I had a slightly better idea than that, or at any rate more elaborate. In one of my conversations with her she mentioned that they owned a rubber dinghy, and then she corrected herself and said they used to own one until Barry started fooling about with it and caused it to capsize. They're such docile children that there seemed to be a slight discrepancy there, as I realised as soon as I met them."

"Even the most docile can be devilish sometimes, but I suppose you think the truth of the matter was that she put her husband's body in this dinghy and sent it for a trip down the river? I must remind you that no dinghy has turned up so far."

"No, but if she'd loosened the screw to allow the air to escape very gradually, just before she launched it, it would have kept afloat long enough for her to push him out a good distance, far enough anyway to get caught in the current before it sank. However, before you raise any more objections, I must tell you that you are preaching to the converted. It's too bad but there it is, because my whole case rested on her being able to drive a car at least adequately enough to cover the mile and a half down to the river without bashing into anything, and that, I am now convinced, is the one thing in the world she could not have done."

"What a blow! But cheer up, Tessa! She could have been fooling you, couldn't she? Pretending not to understand about the gears and so on?"

"So now that I've chucked my theory out of the window you start to pick it up? But it's no use, Robin. I was half prepared for her to put on that sort of act, naturally, and I tried every dodge I knew to catch her out, but she never made a false move. Or rather, she never made a correct one. In the first place, we'd been slogging away for about five minutes and getting absolutely nowhere before I realised her toes were barely brushing the pedals. She happens to be short in the leg, but it turned out that she thought everyone had to drive in those conditions. It had simply not occurred to her that she could push the seat forward. When we'd got that sorted out I kept on at it for about half an hour and she was a jelly of nerves by the end of it, with tears pouring down her face. She kept telling me that she'd been through all this with Mike and that he'd finally had to admit defeat and I believe her, I really do."

"And yet it was her idea to take lessons from a professional?"

"That's true, but I doubt if she's so keen on the idea after this experience. I think I succeeded in destroying what remnants of confidence she had, because up till then she had managed to kid herself that it was as much Mike's fault as hers that she was such a dud."

"And why not? Husbands are notoriously the worst people to teach their wives. Probably he was tight lipped about it and made her more nervous than ever?"

"No, on the contrary. He was obviously rather a sadistic man under that meek and mild manner, but his sadism took rather a novel form. He seems to have destroyed people mainly by kindness. Brenda implied that he never lost his patience during these gruesome driving sessions and that what really unnerved her was the awful sense of inferiority and the knowledge that she was letting her angel down."

"How sad! While he, presumably, had no idea of the effect he was having on her?"

I did not reply to this because the conclusion was so much at variance with my own view of the matter that I was afraid that comment might lead to futile arguments about psychological insights, etcetera, and after an expectant pause Robin continued more seriously:

"Well, I am sorry that one of your cherished theories has to be thrown out, but perhaps it was all for the best.

I must now confess to you that it contained one major flaw which you haven't even heard about yet."

"Why haven't I?"

"Partly because you've hardly given me a chance to tell you. It concerns the actual murder, rather than its aftermath, but it completely rules out the postulation of Mrs Parsons having returned to the house that morning and finding her husband snoring his head off."

"How do you know?"

"Because it defies belief that a man would get up, go out to the garden and begin cutting a hedge, and then become so bored after a few minutes that he downed tools, returned to his bed and promptly fell fast asleep again."

"Hang on a minute! You don't mean to tell me that someone actually saw him clipping the hedge? But how could they have? It's behind the house, so you can't see it from the lane, and it's not overlooked by any of the neighbours. At least, not unless one of them further up the hill happened to be perched on the roof with a telescope."

"No, this wasn't a neighbour. Enquiries among them didn't turn up a thing, as you rightly predicted. This was a much more valuable witness. Name of Peter Wood. The cowman, no less."

"Oh no! Really?"

"Yes, really, and you can see how splendidly he fits the bill? Not only impartial, in so far as he knew both the Parsons by sight, though had never spoken to either of them, but by the very nature of his job he can set the time when he saw Mike to within six or seven minutes."

"Because of the cows, I suppose?"

"Right. Barring electricity cuts and suchlike emergencies, the routine is the same every morning and at nine o'clock, near enough, he brings them back from the milking parlour into the field which adjoins the Parsons' garden. He doesn't have to go right into the field, of course, but the gate is only about fifty yards from the hedge and on the morning in question he had a clear view of Parsons at work on it. And there's something else I must tell you."

"Okay," I sighed. "Spare me nothing, now you've started."

"After he'd been standing there for a few minutes he heard a telephone bell and he saw Parsons drop the shears and run back into the house. I'm sorry, love, but I couldn't have told you all this before. I've only just heard about this Peter Wood myself."

"And he's a reliable witness, I take it?"

"Oh, eminently, I'm afraid. Middle-aged chap, worked for the same farmer for fourteen years, before those new houses were even built."

"So that's the end of that chapter," I said sadly. "We can close it now," and, with a perversity there is no accounting for, had no sooner uttered these words than I began to think about it harder than ever. Somewhere, in something Robin had said, I felt sure lay the key to the whole puzzle. I was convinced of it, even though reconciling myself to the fact that it might be days or even weeks before I hit on it.

"Of course, it doesn't mean dismissing Mrs Parsons entirely," Robin said, as though to console me. "Nothing does that until someone else is proved guilty, but the difficulty with her, along with all the other suspects, great and small, is that so far it has been impossible to establish the time of death, or even to pin it down to within workable limits. Unless it ever becomes known where Parsons went and what he was doing between the time he was seen cutting the hedge and his car turning up outside the pub two or three days later, I can't see that they have a cat's chance of finding the culprit. Unfortunately, the trail was cold long before they got to it and every single lead has simply fizzled out."

It was then that I had one of my blinding flashes, in which not only did the significance of an earlier remark of Robin's come crashing down on me with the force of a sledge hammer, but an entirely new concept of how the murder had been committed rose up before me and clicked into focus.

"Well, perhaps not every single lead has been tried yet," I muttered abstractedly. "There might still be one more which could stand investigating. Now where on earth would one start with that?"

"I can tell you exactly where one would," Robin said sternly. "One would start by going straight to the local coppers who are handling the case and one would tell them everything one knows."

"But I don't know anything, not positively."

"All right then, what one suspects."

"It wouldn't do any good, Robin. I've absolutely no proof, you see. They'd think I was out of my mind, but even if they took me seriously they wouldn't have any more chance than I have of proving it. A good deal less, probably. I'll have to think about it rather carefully before I make a move."

"Where have I heard those words before?" he asked me. "And you know what comes next, don't you?"

"Yes, I think so. You say something like: 'Well, whatever happens, do try and keep out of trouble', and then I say: 'Yes, I promise to, and anyway there's no danger at all.'"

Robin sighed. "We seem to have learnt our parts over the years, if nothing else."

"The difference being," I assured him, "that this time it's true, every word of it. Cross my heart."

CHAPTER TWENTY-ONE

EVER a man whose word was his bond, Gerald came through with the information I had asked for in only a matter of days, although pointing out somewhat reproachfully that Robin could probably have got it for me in half the time.

"Really? You mean our gentleman has a record?"

"It was a long time ago, and he was on the level with you, up to a point. A true blue chartered accountant, right enough. He joined a building society in the Midlands soon after he was qualified. Worked with them for a year or two and then got sent down for fraud and embezzlement. Three years, with six months' remission. It was during the war actually, so it's rather a mystery that he hadn't been called up; but anyway if you've got to spend a few years in jug that's obviously the time to pick for it. No one is going to worry later on about a gap in the references."

"Well, well, fancy that!"

"News to you, eh? Well, naturally, it's not the kind of thing a fellow would be inclined to brag about. I daresay even his best friends don't know."

"As to that," I said, "I wouldn't be too sure. It would never surprise me if there was one who did. Well, thanks a lot, Gerald. I'll have to ring off now because there's a bit of a rumpus going on downstairs."

The rumpus had subsided to a grumbling monotone by the time I reached its source and was emanating from Mrs Cheeseman, our daily help, in the throes of one of her perennial dirges about the revolting behaviour of the younger generation. There are various reasons for resenting her unquestioning assumption that I should necessarily be on her side in this particular conflict, but on this occasion I was ready to concede that she had grounds for complaint. It transpired that she had been bent double over the dustpan and brush on the staircase when her ears were assailed by curious scuffling and rattling sounds behind her, caused, as she soon discovered, by someone trying to push an object through the brass letter box.

Since the morning post had already been delivered, Mrs Cheeseman had instantly concluded, for what reason I cannot tell, that the object in question must either be a bomb or else a revolver aimed at herself. Nevertheless, she had acted with remarkable courage and presence of mind and, taking care to keep out of the line of fire, had crept forward and flung wide the door.

In the brief time she was given to observe him, she managed to ascertain that the messenger was one of those skinny young chaps, with hair falling about all over his face and none too clean with it. She also reported that he had a shifty expression and long finger nails, which was pretty fair going, in view of the fact that she had approximately two seconds to work in. In fact, she had barely got the door open when a small package was thrown down at her feet and almost in the same movement the thrower of it had turned on his heels and bolted down the steps, with his long, dirty hair streaming out behind him, oblivious, so it seemed, to Mrs Cheeseman's shouted commands to come back this instant and tell her what he meant by it.

Leaving the package in situ, she had then started up the stairs, with the intention of making me a party to this outrage, and had collided with me on my way down.

"Shouldn't touch it, if I were you," she advised, as we descended together to the hall. "Best thing would be to pop it in a bucket of water and then ring the Inspector."

Although too bulky to pass through our letter box, it was quite a tiny package, not much bigger than a match box and wrapped in brown paper and string; and there was something instantly familiar in its shape and size, even before I came close enough to see the paper sticker depicting silver wedding bells, with which it was adorned.

"Stop worrying," I told Mrs Cheeseman when she returned to my side a few minutes later with a pail of water, having prudently appropriated this part of the operation for herself. "It was probably only Terry, Frank or Don."

Her censorious attitude did not soften. "As to that, I couldn't say, I'm sure. As I told you, he didn't stop long enough to give me his name. Just threw this thing down and hopped it. Young monkey! Are you going to put it in the bucket before it blows up in our faces?"

It would, of course, have been one way of disposing of it, but only a temporary solution. The truth was that on the very morning when Brenda had first called on me I had been taking part in one of those morning radio shows where, in between a lot of chat about one's personal and public life, listeners' letters are read aloud and their record requests played for them. One of my jobs on that occasion had been to convey best wishes to Paul and Tracey, on their wedding day, from Mum, Dad and Eileen, brothers Terry, Frank and Don, not forgetting Auntie Jill, Tim the budgie and about a hundred others whom I regret to say I have now forgotten. Moreover, at this point in the proceedings the D.J. had given me some fatuous line about how it sounded like such a good party that I was sorry I hadn't been invited and hoped they would send me a slice of wedding cake. The big trouble with a gambit of this kind is that a slice of wedding cake is what you invariably get, and I had not a doubt in the world that this was the work of Paul and Tracey.

It is true that such gifts are not often delivered by hand to the recipient's private residence, but it can happen, and Robin's name and profession had been bandied about a good deal in the course of the programme, so there would not have been the slightest difficulty in finding our address in the telephone directory.

"Stand back!" I instructed Mrs Cheeseman, ripping off the brown paper and the silver paper inside that and finally removing the little white pasteboard box.

When no explosion followed she advanced a step nearer, her expression clouding as she recognised the fading prospect of disaster.

"Hmm! Not very generous, were they?" she said, in a gallant attempt to find something left to disparage. "Won't be able to make a pig of yourself over that little scrap!"

"I don't intend to try," I informed her. "I renounced such things years ago."

Oddly enough, it looked considerably more appetising than the majority of such offerings, but I have to watch my figure and ten o'clock in the morning is no time to dig into a wedge of dried fruit, marzipan and icing sugar, however miniscule. So, having deposited the box on the hall table, I returned to my room and the business of wrestling with the problem of how to fit Gerald's new disclosure into its rightful place in the puzzle.

Mrs Cheeseman did not turn up for work the following day, but there was nothing specially remarkable about that, for she had a hypochondriac husband, and although he usually manages to time his fatal diseases to provide the maximum inconvenience for myself, I forgive her because she really has a very boring life. I have even disciplined myself to listen patiently to a detailed description of his imaginary symptoms and when she arrived at the normal time on the next day I dutifully assumed my sympathetic expression and waited for the dams to burst.

It changed to one of genuine concern, however, when I learnt of the true cause of her absence, for it emerged that it was not the ghastly husband who was responsible this time, but dear old Lassie. This was no laughing matter, for there was nothing fictitious about Lassie's illness and in fact Mrs Cheeseman informed me that she had suffered some kind of heart attack and passed away during the night.

It was hardly a propitious moment to clear up another small mystery which had been plaguing me during the preceding twenty-four hours, but a little later on, when she had dried her tears and reverted to her normal state of grumbling disapproval, I ventured to ask her whether she knew what had become of the box of wedding cake.

"I was going to give it to Robin," I explained. "He has a passion for sweet things, as you know, but when I went to look for it yesterday it had gone."

"Couldn't say, I'm sure. I hope you're not accusing me of taking it?"

"No, of course not. I just thought you might have put it away in a safe place."

"Well, I didn't. Never touched it," Mrs Cheeseman snapped and then turned on the kitchen tap with such ferocity that any further words would literally have been drowned out.

It was so uncharacteristic of her to pass up such a splendid opening for lengthy and pessimistic conjectures that I became rather thoughtful and strongly inclined to believe that it had been just as well that I had not offered Robin the wedding cake. Pondering the matter still more thoroughly during the afternoon, I rejected the idea of telling him the full story, while nevertheless making a mental note to pump him about the effects of cyanide, a commodity which I suspected might very neatly be inserted into a slab of almond icing.

CHAPTER TWENTY-TWO

I REMAINED in a somewhat reflective frame of mind throughout the day, for the longer I dwelt on the sudden demise of poor old Lassie the more sinister the implications appeared.

Two things chiefly disturbed me. The first was that in giving my solemn vow to Robin that I was in no personal danger from Mike's murderer I had been perfectly sincere, and it was distinctly galling to discover that what had started as the unblemished truth should have turned out, in the shortest time imaginable, to be the falsehood of the century. Even more depressing in a sense was the consciousness of having slipped up so badly that the murderer was now actually gunning for me, and yet having no inkling as to when or in what manner I had given myself away. Calculated risks are all very well, but to place oneself in all innocence slap in the way of a violent and painful death is quite another matter and one of the very few consolations to be gleaned from the whole episode was that at least I was innocent no longer and would henceforth be on my guard.

Fortunately for the harmony of our marriage, this sour mood had abated by the time Robin returned, all eager anticipation for the pipe and slippers and plenty of ice in the pink gin, for by then an even bigger crumb of comfort had landed on my plate. It had been deposited there by the very simple deduction that it merely required a little delving back into the events of the preceding days to discover exactly how I had betrayed more knowledge than I should rightly have possessed and that the answer, when it turned up, would provide positive proof of the murderer's identity.

I had arrived at this consoling conclusion after a period of solid, concentrated thought and found it so impeccably logical that my one regret was in not being able to share it with Robin. However, he was suitably forthcoming on the subject of death by cyanide poisoning and not unduly curious about my motives in questioning him and, by the time we had seized the rare opportunity for an early night and gone upstairs to bed, I felt reasonably confident that a few hours' sleep would banish all the confusions and get my memory back into proper working order.

It was rather weird in a way, because everything turned out so entirely differently. I had only just started to remove my make-up when Robin came sauntering back from his dressing room, saying in a plaintive voice:

"How did this monstrosity get into my wardrobe, do you know?"

He was standing behind me, outside my line of vision as I pulled faces at myself in the mirror, slapping on the cold cream and I said:

"What's the matter? Has Mrs Cheeseman been up to her tricks again?" before swivelling round to get a look at the monstrosity.

It was a blue and red striped dressing gown and the instant I laid eyes on it I became totally transfixed, while my mind went into action so fast that it was a wonder that the whirring noises weren't audible all over the room.

"I suppose she was responsible," Robin answered, still eyeing the dressing gown with deep revulsion, "but you'd think even she would know it's not my style, not to mention about four sizes too small. Where on earth do you suppose she found it?"

He doesn't find me particularly attractive at this stage of the demaquillage and had doubtless deliberately kept his face averted from mine, but something unnatural in my posture may have got through to him, for all at once he looked up in alarm and came forward, flinging Mike's dressing gown on to a chair on his way.

"What's up, Tessa? Are you all right?"

"Oh yes, fine, perfectly all right," I answered in a light-headed way.

"You don't look it, you look terrible, but perhaps it's just that mess on your face. Why are you goggling at me in that insane fashion, though? And why don't you answer me, for God's sake?"

"Because you keep asking all the wrong questions," I explained. "This is where you're supposed to say: 'You look as though you'd seen a ghost', and then I say, 'Yes, I believe I have.'"

"Right. Let's carry on from there. Whose ghost?"

"Mike Parsons, of course."

"Ah! And did he tell you how he met his death?"

"Naturally."

"And so now you know it all?"

"Well, not quite all, because there were one or two things which Mike didn't know himself, but I think we shall soon get them; or at any rate Superintendent Meiklejohn will. We could give him two lines of enquiry to follow up straight away. One is to find out who owns the Four Corners Travel Bureau and the other is to check with some of the banks in the locality to see whether Brenda has opened a separate account in her own name."

"Be good enough to settle one personal matter first," Robin said.

"What's that?"

"Is this going to be a long story?"

"I'm afraid so," I replied.

"Then would you mind if I went downstairs and got myself a whisky and soda before you begin?"

"Not at all. You can bring me one at the same time."

"On one condition."

"Oh yes?"

"That you'll have wiped all that goo off your face by the time I return."

I did better than that, as it happened, for during the interval I lined up all the items I had to tell him and slotted them into the right order, which meant that after all it was still only midnight when we went to bed.

I was glad about this because, purely for my own satisfaction, there was one final piece of business to be undertaken before the police took over and by eight o'clock the next morning I was already driving out of London to pay my very last call on Brenda.

CHAPTER TWENTY-THREE

"I AM all in favour of Women's Lib, as you both know," Toby said crossly. "But I consider this was going too far."

"Although you could say it was one up to the movement, in a sense. I mean, who would have believed that two such different women could sink their personalities to unite in a common goal, especially something so tricky as murder? It just shows that no field should be barred to us on grounds of temperament."

"And perhaps you are priding yourself on the fact that it took another woman to bring them down?" Robin suggested.

"No, far from it. I was bang in the centre of things from the word go and still they fooled me completely. I never could get round the fact that each of them made a perfect fifty per cent suspect. It took me ages to see that by joining them together you could make one all rounder. And you must admit they did a splendid job. The pretence of one of them never having heard of the second, and of the second despising what she'd heard of the first was quite masterly. All the more convincing for never being overdone."

"I do rather agree with you, Tessa," Toby admitted. "It was quite a triumph to keep up the pretence while planning such a complicated programme. I wonder how the idea came to them in the first place? Some kind of extra-sensory perception, do you suppose? Did they communicate by thought waves?"

"No, I think they must have met once while Mike was alive, although probably only once, and it was sheer fluke that nobody ever knew about it, because I imagine it was during that meeting that the plan was first mooted. After that, they only kept in touch by telephone, probably using a code of some kind, in case the lines should be crossed."

"But what brought them together in the first place, if the plot was only hatched after they met?"

"Oh, that's easy. Don't you remember Robin telling us how amazed he was that Chloe hadn't tried to enlist Brenda's help in restraining Mike when he became such a nuisance? I stupidly dismissed the notion because I'd decided that Brenda was so effectively marooned in her suburban ivory tower that it would have been pretty hard to contact her, even if one had wanted to. But I should have realised that this situation was not of her own choice. It was simply one of Mike's manoeuvres for keeping her totally under his thumb. It's true that she did deliberately shun the neighbours, but that was because she was well aware of the stories he had spread about her being a slattern and an alcoholic and she felt humiliated by their pity and disapproval. But I am quite sure that she would have welcomed overtures from the people he worked with. She hated being kept out of all that side of his life."

"Wasn't he spreading exactly the same stories round the studios?"

"I'm sure he was, but he may not have succeeded quite so well there. I think that was why he took her to the Christmas Eve party. Normally he didn't allow her within miles of the studios, but perhaps his credibility was wearing thin, so he dusted Brenda off and brought her out on that occasion purely to demonstrate what a hard case she was."

"You're not suggesting that he actually contrived to get her drunk in public in order to boost his own verisimilitude? I find that very hard to believe."

"So do I," Robin agreed. "And I think Tessa must have got her facts a bit muddled here. I wouldn't have said it was possible to pass one's wife off to the world as a confirmed alcoholic unless there was some truth in it."

"But of course there was some truth in it, Robin. I don't deny that for a second."

"Meaning that she had occasional bouts?"

"No, I mean that she's cured of it, but only to the point where she can't take a drop of alcohol in any shape or form. She's one of those people who, once they start drinking, are unable to stop. Mike knew that as well as anyone and he talked her into having a couple of stiff ones before they set out for the party, on the grounds that it would liven her up and release all the terrible inhibitions. He even took a flask along in the car, believe it or not, so she was pretty far gone when they arrived. What the little brute didn't realise was that he'd finally gone too far and the worm was about to turn. About to turn into a clever and determined murderess, as you might say."

"Is that when she decided to kill him?"

"I think I'd have done the same," Toby admitted. "She certainly had provocation, you know. Perhaps we should arrange for Gerald to get her acquitted?"

"He may have a little difficulty there," Robin pointed out, "since it would appear that she has confessed."

"Only to me, and I advised her not to say a word unless her solicitor was present. But would you both care to hear the whole story, exactly as she told it to me this morning?"

"Very much indeed," Toby replied. "Shouldn't we, Robin?"

"Since you know as well as I do that Tessa means to tell us anyway, I suppose you feel there is nothing to be lost by being gracious about it?"

"It all began," I said, ignoring this, "almost seven years ago, soon after the birth of Barry Parsons when Brenda first began to hit the bottle. Up to then her life hadn't been too awful because although Mike neglected her shamefully she was at least able to go out and about on her own a bit and she also had a part time job. Once there was a baby in the house all that came to an end. He'd completely destroyed her confidence for driving and so she was stranded on her own in the house from eight o'clock in the morning, quite often until ten or eleven at night, and sometimes all through the weekend as well.

"When Mike discovered that she was consoling herself with a steady intake of whisky and gin the most extraordinary thing happened. Instead of doing everything in his power to cut off her supplies, as most husbands would, and which wouldn't have been at all difficult in their circumstances, he positively encouraged her to step up her drinking. He even arranged for a dozen bottles to be delivered to the house every week, so that she would no longer have the trouble of pushing the pram down to the supermarket for it. And you know why? I'll tell you."

"We thought you might."

"Because under that shy little exterior he was a sadist and a power maniac. He wanted to dominate people totally and to do it he had first to reduce them to the meanest abject level. Brenda's weakness made a perfect weapon because he would arrive home and find her slightly groggy, and the house not quite so trim as he felt it should be, and so then the bullying and scolding would begin. Sometimes he would go on for over an hour, until she was a sobbing wreck, swearing over and over again that she would never touch another drop. You get the picture?"

"Clearly," Toby said with extreme distaste.

"It doesn't get any brighter, I must tell you, because when he'd wrung that situation dry he'd suddenly turn on the smiles again and tell her that she was forgiven, but she must take it easy for a bit and put her feet up while he cleared up some of the mess. Then he'd set to with the brushes and vacuum cleaner and literally force her to sit by, twiddling her thumbs, and watch him do the house-work. Afterwards he'd tell her she was a good girl and should have a nice strong nightcap, to make sure she slept well, and off they'd toddle to bed.

"Actually, at this stage, Brenda wasn't too bad, just hardly ever completely sober, and this went on even when she became pregnant again. But of course those two particular conditions tend to make women rather a drag and inevitably Mike grew bored with tormenting her and spent even less time at home. I gather it was around then that he first took up with Chloe and her brother.

"So naturally Brenda became worse and worse until finally the catastrophe hit them. It was when Keith, the younger child, was about two years old. Brenda was at the end of her tether, coping with two small children in solitary confinement and the drinking had got a real hold on her. One day, as the direct result of her being half stoned, the baby fell on to the electric fire and ended up in hospital with third degree burns.

"Well, as you might guess, that brought matters to a head. The little boy was in a touch and go condition for weeks and when the doctor sniffed out the true cause of the accident he prevailed on Brenda to go as a voluntary patient for treatment. She'd had the most appalling shock and didn't need much persuasion. Whether Mike was quite so ready to fall in with the idea I don't know, but I daresay it had shaken him a bit too, and anyway he probably had no option, especially as his sister-in-law was quite prepared to have Barry to stay with her in the meantime. I don't think she's such a bad woman, incidentally, but like so many others she's utterly ignorant of the real nature of Brenda's complaint and inclined to take a very moralising attitude."

"One way and another, they sound a thoroughly detestable family," Toby remarked.

"Yes, and isn't it strange how things are so rarely what they seem? You bowl through the night in a train, looking at all the little lighted windows and you picture people behind them, watching television or planning their summer holidays over steaming cups of cocoa, and it all seems so safe and cosy. I quite envy them sometimes, but of course it isn't really like that at all. Half of them are in the grip of these terrible primitive emotions and working them out on each other in the most fiendish ways imaginable."

"A trifle less of the homespun philosophy, if you please!" Toby entreated. "We haven't got all night, you know. At least, I haven't."

"Oh, very well," I said. "And it may please you to know that we can skip a year or two here, because we now move on to that studio party. The baby has recovered, although he's still physically retarded and has such a terrifying squint that it's quite painful to look at him; and a combination of fright and medical treatment has done the trick for Brenda too. She is now on the wagon.

"Well, you know what took place at the party and of course the next morning she was nearly out of her mind. It wasn't only that she had the most ghastly hangover and was craving for a drink to set her up again. She also had to face the fact that Mike had done this to her deliberately, that he actively sought to turn her into an addict again, even though it would lead to her total destruction and possibly the children's as well. Some fun, eh?

"Incidentally," I went on, as neither of them answered, "that was one of the two points where Chloe gave herself away, if only I'd been bright enough to notice. She hinted that the reason for Mike being teetotal was that it was he who had caused an accident when drunk, whereas every single other person who knew him maintained that it was on account of his wife's dipsomania. Chloe, of course, was the exception who knew the whole truth, but that was one part of the story which she and Brenda hadn't worked on."

"What was the other?" Robin asked.

"Oh, that was the mythical Sandy who kept me running round in circles for so long. Brenda had invented him, for reasons which I'll come to in a moment, but she knew I would get to Chloe as soon as I saw the scrap of paper with her signature on it. In fact, that was her sole purpose in showing it to me."

"Which strikes me as odd. One would have thought their best bet was to keep you apart?"

"Yes, I expect that was the original policy, but I don't think Brenda had bargained on my taking up her cause with quite such zeal. Instead of the passive role she'd allotted me I had started ringing her up and even driving down to see her without proper warning. It didn't suit her, and Chloe was brought in to demonstrate that even though his wife had no motive for wanting him out of the way plenty of other people might have, and at the same time to discourage me from getting too nosey. However, that was a last minute strategy and when she set it up Brenda forgot to warn Chloe about this fictitious Sandy. What happened was that when I called at Old Lock Cottage, Chloe first of all denied ever having heard of any Sandy, but while I was talking to her someone rang up, and then a bit later on she quite casually threw it out that she did remember Mike mentioning him. It was curious and I should have realised earlier that this was a common factor between them. They both knew about Sandy, whereas everyone else I questioned had simply never heard of him.

"However, to get back to Brenda's story, it was when the frightful truth about Mike dawned on her that she made up her mind sooner or later to kill him. She hadn't the faintest idea how she would do it, still less how to do it and get away with it, but she hit on a very clever jumping off point. It occurred to her that she had a unique weapon and without quite knowing how she would use it she determined to make it a secret weapon. Poor old Brenda, I believe she might have been quite a brainy type if she'd had a proper education. I expect there must be thousands of women like her, don't you? All their latent intelligence turning to cunning, simply because they've never had a proper outlet for it or a chance to develop it constructively."

"Oh, all right," I said crossly, as Toby held up a warning hand. "If you want the story straight and without the interesting sidelights you shall have it. Brenda's secret weapon was her drinking. Or, to be precise, her pretence of drinking. She never let the act get too ambitious, but she knew better than most how to imitate someone in a mild state of intoxication and she was very careful to neglect the house a bit, specially when she knew for certain that Mike would be coming home. It was all deliberately done to ensure that he would consistently underestimate her and so be off his guard when her moment came. She even kept up the farce of the weekly order. I do wish I'd remembered to ask her what she did with all those bottles. Perhaps she managed to flog them. Somehow I can't see her pouring all that expensive stuff down the drain. She's a very frugal person."

"Not only frugal and clever, but superhuman too, if you ask me," Robin said. "Imagine someone with a weakness like hers spending day after day alone in the house, with all that temptation within reach and not even a spot of housework to keep her busy!"

"Ah, but you see she didn't spend all that time alone in the house. Oh dear me, no, you underestimate her. I should explain that she was practical as well as clever and she got herself a job. Only part time, admittedly, and it was understood that she couldn't work during the school holidays or when her husband was at home for any reason, but can't you see what a delightful set-up it was? Once the boys had been despatched on the school bus all she had to do was to trot down to an office in the High Street and earn herself a dinky private income, which was tucked away in a separate account for the rainy, or rather sunny, day when she became a widow. No need to bother with the boring old cooking and housework because she only had to put on a show of being slightly squiffy and the little man would see to all that in the evening."

"Did she really tell you this herself?"

"It was more a question of confirming it for me. I'd had my suspicions for some time, partly because of all the tricks she'd resorted to to ensure that I would only tele-phone her by arrangement. First of all she spun a pitiful tale about hating to answer the telephone in case it should be Mike, and then she was so upset and disappointed when it turned out not to be. She couldn't keep that up once he was known to be dead, so then we had the one about being too frightened to answer because of the anonymous calls. Quite untrue, of course, but having invented this Sandy in order to strew a few false trails around, she used him again as one of her anonymous callers. Unfortunately for her, this was a double-edged sword. I had urged her to tell the police about these calls and eventually she did so, possibly fearing that otherwise I might, and it had a repercussion she hadn't bargained for. They told her they were going to tap her line, which meant that from then on it became too risky for her and Chloe to keep in touch by telephone. They had to find another means and luckily there was a perfect one ready made for them. I speak now of the Four Corners Travel Bureau."

"You have been getting around, haven't you, Tessa?" Robin asked reproachfully.

"It's only fifteen minutes' walk from Hill Grove, actually. I saw Chloe coming out of it the other day, behaving in a somewhat furtive manner and when I confronted her with it she denied it absolutely."

"I can hardly see how admitting it would have incriminated her," Toby said. "But no doubt you are about to tell us?"

"Because an office at the back of it was where Brenda did her accounting and secretarial work. Chloe had once revealed that her mother had left her part share in an agency. She didn't specify what kind, but I put two and two together trusting to luck they'd add up to five and that, my friends, was the first major breakthrough.

"Well, I see from your faces," I went on after a brief silence, "that you still do not see the vital importance of sniffing out a collaboration between Chloe and Brenda. Apart from Alec Ferguson, who was a candidate at one time, those two were always my principal suspects."

"Why Ferguson?"

"He became so touchy and evasive as soon as Mike was known to have vanished; really vanished, I mean, not just left his wife in the lurch. And then he threw up his job for no apparent reason. However, with a little help from Gerald, I soon realised that he was scared stiff that there would be a police enquiry at the studios, which he might become involved in, particularly as there's reason to suppose that Mike was blackmailing him. All he wanted was to lie low until the thing had blown over.

"So anyway, there I was with Brenda and Chloe once more, each of them temperamentally capable of such a crime, but physically having to be ruled out. One of them had a first rate motive, which she didn't hesitate to proclaim at the top of her lungs, but no opportunity, for you cannot by any stretch of the imagination conceive of a dead man being shoved in the river in such a way that he will float upstream for twelve or fifteen miles. The other, being his wife, had the best opportunity for murdering him, though no perceptible motive and, as I discovered during the driving lesson, no hope at all of getting the corpse into the river. The minute I got a hint that they were in it together all these little problems were smoothed away."

"If you really picked up all this as you went along, I cannot think why you didn't pass it on to the proper quarters," Robin said, being subject to a one track mind on occasions.

"There wasn't anything to pass on; just a growing pile of trivial incidents and anomalies which didn't fall into a pattern. Take that business of the wheelbarrow, for instance. It happened when I met Brenda for only the second time, long before any of us knew that Mike was dead, and yet if I'd played it right she might have broken down there and then and confessed all. Just for a flash she believed I'd guessed the truth and she came within an inch of admitting it."

"What was the incident of the wheelbarrow?" Toby asked. "Did you not tell me, or can I have forgotten?"

"Or could it be that you weren't listening? It was when I was leaving. The little boys were giving each other rides in the wheelbarrow. Brenda went through the roof and screamed at them like a lunatic. Afterwards she practically passed out and I said something like, 'I suppose it was seeing the wheelbarrow that upset you?', to which she replied, 'How did you guess?' and if only I'd kept my silly mouth shut I might have learnt exactly what it was about the wheelbarrow that sent her into hysterics, thereby saving myself a whole lot of trouble."

"And exactly what was it about the wheelbarrow?"

"I think there were two things really. One was that it had been used as a prop in the hedge clipping scene, which was set up to establish her alibi and to confuse everyone about the time of Mike's death. But what really gave her the horrors was that she and Chloe had used it the night before to wheel him from the house to the garage, and I daresay she hasn't been able to look at it since without seeing his dead body curled up inside it."

"So he was actually killed the night before his so-called disappearance, was he?"

"Yes, and that was the one part of the plan which had to be left to chance. All the rest had been worked out to a hair, but it was agreed that Brenda should choose her own moment for lacing his bedtime drink and holding the cushion over his face as soon as he'd passed out. Funny how enormous events hinge on tiny ones, isn't it? It was a dry, moonless night, which made it suitable, but what chiefly spurred her on was that he'd drawn all the money out of their joint account and was proposing to squander the lot on some silly boat. She was sick to death of his chucking his money around on his stupid good works and on spirits which nobody drank, and this was the last straw."

"So having killed him, then what?"

"Immediately rang up Chloe, who gave her brother a treble dose of his sleeping pills, locked him in the house and drove herself up to Hill Grove. She parked her car under a tree on the verge between the lane and the field and walked the rest of the way to Number 32. She and Brenda dumped Mike in the wheelbarrow and placed it in the back of his own car, barrow and all, and the rubber dinghy on top. Between one and two in the morning they all went down the Strand and when it was silent and deserted, in he went, the only slight hitch being the lost punt pole.

"After that it was simply a question of their walking back separately to Hill Grove, where Chloe collected her car and drove home, arriving there well before daylight. Brenda, having snatched a few hours' sleep, got up at her usual time, locking her bedroom door behind her. As soon as the boys had left on the bus she nipped back home, put on Mike's dressing gown and began clipping the hedge. In an incautious moment she had told me that whenever he had a day off he liked to take it easy and potter about in the garden before he had his bath. Very likely Peter Wood, the cowman, had never seen him in anything else but a dressing gown, and the clockwork system with the cows cuts both ways, you know. Brenda knew exactly what time the man would bring them back into the field and Chloe knew exactly what time to tele-phone so that he would hear the outside bell. As soon as it rang Brenda bolted indoors, removed the dressing gown and scurried down to the supermarket, where she probably spent about five minutes instead of the half hour she claimed."

"And what about the poor dotty brother? Was Robin right about its being a genuine suicide?"

"You know, I have my theories about that too, though they obviously can't be proved. I believe he did kill himself, either purposely or by accident, but of course that shot Chloe straight into the limelight, which was the last thing she wanted, so to get the matter bundled out of sight as rapidly as possible she decided to remove any doubts that it was suicide. Hence the note, which I am sure was a forgery. After all, you need to be exceptionally skilful with the hand and eye to hold down her sort of job in the art department, and I'm not at all impressed by the experts' findings. In fact I'd have had more faith in them if they'd come up with the opposite conclusion because the boy's handwriting would certainly have deteriorated after his operation. However, what really convinces me that Chloe fixed it is the fact that the note was addressed to the coroner. She told me Johnnie had been mentally retarded all his life and I very much doubt if he would have known of the existence of such a person, far less what his functions were. People so often ditch themselves by adding these fancy bits."

"Well, I suppose we must allow you that one little side-light on human frailty," Toby said. "Although I trust it will be the last; and personally I feel it was Brenda who made the worst miscalculation. Poor woman, how she must be regretting the impulse to bring her sad story to you!"

"I wonder why she did?" Robin asked.

"I don't feel it was an impulse exactly. I believe she wanted to establish herself as a creature demented with grief and worry because her husband had walked out on her. It's rather difficult to do that when you know as few people as she does, and in many respects I was the ideal confidante. She could practise her story on me and make sure she'd got it pat, in the event of having to repeat it in a police station, and there was a good chance too that through me she'd manage to pick up a few tips as to which way the official minds were working. It wasn't a bad idea and I might never have been able to prove anything against her if it hadn't been for the dressing gown. When Robin walked in with it last night I suddenly remembered that it had been hanging over my arm when I met Chloe in the car park and she must have thought I was flaunting it at her deliberately, to show that I knew she was in the plot. I didn't of course, but that was why . . ."

"Why what?" Robin asked, pouncing on the hesitation .

"Why she was so angry," I replied, recollecting myself. I had been about to explain that that was why Chloe and Brenda had decided I was becoming a danger to them and why Brenda, with a little help from her friend and the studio wardrobe, had impersonated Terry, Frank or Don, in order to deliver a slice of poisoned wedding cake. However, Robin's next words made me even more thankful that I had stopped in time.

"I wonder," he said, looking at me in a very wondering way. "I really do wonder that, knowing all this, you should still have taken it into your head to go and visit her at home this morning. Some people would have called it risky."

"I didn't visit her at home. I called at the Four Corners Travel Bureau, where I guessed she would be, and I said: 'The police are now moving in on 32, Hill Grove and I've come to take you out for coffee and one last piece of advice.'"

Robin seemed reasonably satisfied by this explanation, but it certainly was a shame that, having sworn to him that I was in no danger, I could not now very well own up to the wedding cake incident. I think it rounds off the story rather neatly, and I am still hoping that the right moment will come to tell him about it.

THE END

THE detective novels of Anne Morice seem rather to reflect the actual life and background of the author, whose full married name was Felicity Anne Morice Worthington Shaw. Felicity was born in the county of Kent on February 18, 1916, one of four daughters of Harry Edward Worthington, a well-loved village doctor, and his pretty young wife, Muriel Rose Morice. Seemingly this is an unexceptional provenance for an English mystery writer—yet in fact Felicity's complicated ancestry was like something out of a classic English mystery, with several cases of children born on the wrong side of the blanket to prominent sires and their humbly born paramours. Her mother Muriel Rose was the natural daughter of dressmaker Rebecca Garnett Gould and Charles John Morice, a Harrow graduate and footballer who played in the 1872 England/Scotland match. Doffing his football kit after this triumph, Charles became a stockbroker like his father, his brothers and his nephew Percy John de Paravicini, son of Baron James Prior de Paravicini and Charles' only surviving sister, Valentina Antoinette Sampayo Morice. (Of Scottish mercantile origin, the Morices had extensive Portuguese business connections.) Charles also found time, when not playing the fields of sport or commerce, to father a pair of out-of-wedlock children with a coachman's daughter, Clementina Frances Turvey, whom he would later marry.

Her mother having passed away when she was only four years old, Muriel Rose was raised by her half-sister Kitty, who had wed a commercial traveler, at the village of Birchington-on-Sea, Kent, near the city of Margate.

There she met kindly local doctor Harry Worthington when he treated her during a local measles outbreak. The case of measles led to marriage between the physician and his patient, with the couple wedding in 1904, when Harry was thirty-six and Muriel Rose but twenty-two. Together Harry and Muriel Rose had a daughter, Elizabeth, in 1906. However Muriel Rose's three later daughters—Angela, Felicity and Yvonne—were fathered by another man, London playwright Frederick Leonard Lonsdale, the author of such popular stage works (many of them adapted as films) as *On Approval* and *The Last of Mrs. Cheyney* as well as being the most steady of Muriel Rose's many lovers.

Unfortunately for Muriel Rose, Lonsdale's interest in her evaporated as his stage success mounted. The playwright proposed pensioning off his discarded mistress with an annual stipend of one hundred pounds apiece for each of his natural daughters, provided that he and Muriel Rose never met again. The offer was accepted, although Muriel Rose, a woman of golden flights and fancies who romantically went by the name Lucy Glitters (she told her daughters that her father had christened her with this appellation on account of his having won a bet on a horse by that name on the day she was born), never got over the rejection. Meanwhile, "poor Dr. Worthington" as he was now known, had come down with Parkinson's Disease and he was packed off with a nurse to a cottage while "Lucy Glitters," now in straitened financial circumstances by her standards, moved with her daughters to a maisonette above a cake shop in Belgravia, London, in a bid to get the girls established. Felicity's older sister Angela went into acting for a profession, and her mother's theatrical ambition for her daughter is said to have been the inspiration for Noel Coward's amusingly imploring 1935 hit song "Don't Put Your Daughter on the Stage, Mrs. Worthington." Angela's greatest contribution to the cause of thespianism by far came when she married actor and theatrical agent Robin Fox, with whom she produced England's Fox acting dynasty, including her sons Edward and James and grandchildren Laurence, Jack, Emilia and Freddie.

Felicity meanwhile went to work in the office of the GPO Film Unit, a subdivision of the United Kingdom's General Post Office established in 1933 to produce documentary films. Her daughter Mary Premila Boseman has written that it was at the GPO Film Unit that the "pretty and fashionably slim" Felicity met documentarian Alexander Shaw—"good looking, strong featured, dark haired and with strange brown eyes between yellow and green"—and told herself "that's the man I'm going to marry," which she did. During the Thirties and Forties Alex produced and/or directed over a score of prestige documentaries, including *Tank Patrol, Our Country* (introduced by actor Burgess Meredith) and *Penicillin.* After World War Two Alex worked with the United Nations agencies UNESCO and UNRWA and he and Felicity and their three children resided in developing nations all around the world. Felicity's daughter Mary recalls that Felicity "set up house in most of these places adapting to each circumstance. Furniture and curtains and so on were made of local materials. . . . The only possession that followed us everywhere from England was the box of Christmas decorations, practically heirlooms, fragile and attractive and unbroken throughout.

In Wad Medani in the Sudan they hung on a thorn bush and looked charming."

It was during these years that Felicity began writing fiction, eventually publishing two fine mainstream novels, *The Happy Exiles* (1956) and *Sun-Trap* (1958). The former novel, a lightly satirical comedy of manners about British and American expatriates in an unnamed British colony during the dying days of the Empire, received particularly good reviews and was published in both the United Kingdom and the United States, but after a nasty bout with malaria and the death, back in England, of her mother Lucy Glitters, Felicity put writing aside for more than a decade, until under her pseudonym Anne Morice, drawn from her two middle names, she successfully launched her Tessa Crichton mystery series in 1970. "From the royalties of these books," notes Mary Premila Boseman, "she was able to buy a house in Hambleden, near Henley-on-Thames; this was the first of our houses that wasn't rented." Felicity spent a great deal more time in the home country during the last two decades of her life, gardening and cooking for friends (though she herself when alone subsisted on a diet of black coffee and watercress) and industriously spinning her tales of genteel English murder in locales much like that in which she now resided. Sometimes she joined Alex in his overseas travels to different places, including Washington, D.C., which she wrote about with characteristic wryness in her 1977 detective novel *Murder with Mimicry* ("a nice lively book saturated with show business," pronounced the *New York Times Book Review*). Felicity Shaw lived a full life of richly varied experiences, which are rewardingly reflected in her books, the last of